HEALING WATER

Healing Water

A HAWAIIAN STORY

Joyce Moyer Hostetter

CALKINS CREEK
Honesdale, Pennsylvania

LIBRARY OF CONGRESS CATALOGING-IN-PUBLICATION DATA
Hostetter, Joyce.
Healing water : a Hawaiian story / Joyce Moyer Hostetter.
p. cm.
Summary: When teenaged Pia is sent to Hawaii's leprosy settlement
on Molokai Island in the 1860s, he chooses anger and self-reliance
as his means of survival, but the faithful example of other villagers
and one remarkable priest threaten to destroy his desire for revenge.
ISBN 978-1-59078-514-0 (hardcover : alk. paper)
[1. Leprosy—Fiction. 2. Conduct of life—Fiction.
3. Molokai (Hawaii)—History—19th century—Fiction.
4. Hawaii—History—To 1893—Fiction.] I. Title.
PZ7.H81125He 2008
[Fic]—dc22
2007018349

CALKINS CREEK
An Imprint of Boyds Mills Press, Inc.
815 Church Street
Honesdale, Pennsylvania 18431

To all who serve, wherever you are!

One's Molokai can be anywhere.
—Brother Joseph Dutton,
who served in Hawaii's leprosy settlement for forty-four years

C O N T

ENTS

I

Ma'i Ho'oka'awale
[THE SEPARATING SICKNESS]

The sheriff led us like criminals through the streets of Honolulu. A deputy walked beside me. I heard the squish of mud beneath his boots and I saw his large shape from the corner of my eye. But I did not look up.

My mother would be somewhere in the crowd. And my little sister, Kimi, and Kamaka's mother, and Tūtū, his grandmother.

This time, surely Kamaka himself would be there.

I was desperate to see them all. But shame kept my eyes on the ground. I could not bear to see the grief and pity on their faces.

It didn't matter whether the people who watched us knew my name or the names of the other unfortunates with me. They still reached out with hands of compassion.

But the deputies pushed them back. "Don't touch!" they snapped.

Did the officials know how long it had been since anyone had touched me?

I could tell when we were nearing the harbor because I could hear the busyness. Wagons clattered on the street and horses neighed. Vendors called out the prices they wanted for their goods. Children giggled as they chased each other through the crowd.

The people who had gathered to watch expressed their shock in languages I did not understand. I knew the English and Hawaiian but could catch only a word or two of those languages from China, Japan, and the various places in Europe.

From somewhere nearby, I heard the pounding of hammers and the voices of workmen calling out to each other. They were probably building a new store for foreign wares, or maybe it was another grog shop where whalers could quench their thirst for strong drink. I didn't look to see what the building was. It didn't matter; I would never see it again.

Already I could feel Honolulu becoming more and more like a foreign land to me.

The sheriff led us to the wharf, and suddenly the sounds of the city were swallowed up by the loud wails of our families. The deputies turned then, and without lifting my head I knew they were receiving gifts for us. Our families had brought woven sleeping mats, wrapped parcels, and wooden crates filled with supplies.

And, of course, flower garlands to show their *aloha*.

A deputy pushed a gray woolen bundle into my hands. He put sweet and spicy-smelling garlands over my shoulder. I looked up then, and there they were—my *'ohana*. And Kamaka's family, too. Their wet faces were twisted with pain.

When my mother saw me look at her, she could not stay away from me. She slipped beneath the rope that separated us from the crowd. Seeing that the deputies were busy with parcels and flower garlands, she pulled me to her and put her round face so close to mine that her tears washed my cheeks. "Don't forget us, Pia, my child," she pleaded. "Write to us. We will write to you. And send you food and clothing."

For once, I did not protest being called a child. For the first time, I did not want to be full-grown like Kamaka. Or strong like him, or anything at all like him. I just wanted to be a child in my mother's arms. I wept into her softness.

But then they grabbed her. My mother tightened her grip and

I heard her pitiful wailing. A deputy pulled me toward the boat and my mother pulled me toward home. I clutched her arms and felt her sleeves rip from her dress as the officer dragged me away.

"No!" my mother screamed. "Pia! My only son!"

A second deputy put his hands on me. I could feel only my mother's fingers now, her nails dragging through my hands. Then we lost each other.

She collapsed on the street. I wanted to lift her up, to put the sunshine back in her round face again. But I could do nothing. They dragged me up the plank and onto the ship. Her screams followed me, pulling me back.

But the steamboat chugged impatiently and a deputy pushed me into the cattle hold. Other passengers shoved against me, trying to get to the ship's edge, hoping for one last glimpse of O'ahu island and the people who loved us.

I pushed through the elbows to get to the rail. I had to see my mother again. And Kimi. There she was, my sweet sister, slumped in the sand with Yellow Cat in her arms. I saw Kamaka's family, Lani and Tūtū, holding my mother between them. Rocking her back and forth. Joining their cries with hers.

I felt the churning of the propellers and the movement of the steamer beneath us. The ship pulled me away from our home, ripping me like bark from a tree. A woman beside me removed a *lei* from her shoulders and tossed it over the railing. It floated alone on the wide water for a moment until someone else did the same and others followed.

Garland by garland they tossed reds and oranges, purples and yellows in the blue-green water. Together they were like one of Hawai'i's rainbows floating across our harbor. I ripped a *lei* from my neck and threw it into the stream of flowers. I watched it drift back to shore. If it arrived, then I too might return someday ...

I prayed that Kamaka would see it. I prayed that *I* would see Kamaka.

But God did not answer my prayers. I searched every face in the crowd on shore—and none of them was Kamaka's. I could not have missed him, so tall and broad with his fine face, laughing eyes, and curly hair.

I turned away from Oʻahu and pushed back through the elbows crowding the rail. There was an empty space at the front of the cattle hold. The deck was spattered with mud and cow dung, but in that moment I didn't care about being clean. I would wash when I got to Molokaʻi. I slid onto the deck and bowed my head onto my knees. One of the deputies shoved my parcel of provisions at me. I must have dropped it while saying goodbye to my mother. I hung on to it because it smelled smoky and sweet, like home, and because I would not be able to survive without it.

Soon after, a man grabbed my arm, and before I knew what he was doing, he yanked me to my feet. He thrust his face up to mine. Up close like this I could see how leprosy was changing his face. Did I look like that?

I felt my own cheeks. My fingers found no lumps. But how long would it take? How long until I was afraid to see myself in someone else's eyes?

"Come." The man dragged me to the ship's railing. "Jump overboard with me. We will swim to shore and hide in the hills." He glanced around and lowered his voice. "The guards will relax their watch soon. After we pass Diamond Head, let's slip over the side of the ship and lose ourselves in the waves. We'll hide among the rocks and climb the cliffs when it gets dark. We can live inside the crater while we gather provisions and make our plans."

I said nothing. The man gave me a shake.

"What do you say? You look like a strong one. You could

climb Diamond Head in the dark." He grabbed my head and turned it so that I could not miss our ancient volcano.

My throat ached at the sight of that faithful hill. I'd climbed it so many times with Kamaka. Now it stood there like a silent soldier, saluting my passage into death.

I was ready to turn away when I saw a movement at the top of Diamond Head. A horse, a white horse made golden by the setting sun, was outlined against the blue sky. A rider sat upon the horse's back, as motionless and as familiar as the hill itself.

Kamaka! From his high and untouchable perch—with not so much as a wave—Kamaka watched my passing.

I wondered what he was thinking. Did he consider me dead already?

My grief turned to anger then.

I thrust my shoulder against the man who wanted me to climb Diamond Head. "Leave me alone!"

I shoved again, harder this time, sending him backward onto the ship's deck. "Diamond Head?" I screamed. "If you could swim to shore you wouldn't have the strength to crawl onto the sand. You're as good as dead already. And you are, too!" I shouted to a little girl with a thin face and wide eyes. I tried not to notice that she looked like my sister. "And you and you and you!" I pointed at anyone who dared to stare at me. "You're going to die—all of you. Your grave is waiting on Moloka'i!"

I screamed awful, angry things I would be ashamed to remember later. I screamed the things I felt about myself. That *my* death awaited me. That *I* was helpless to do anything to rescue myself. And that all of these people suffered the same fate.

I kicked and punched and abused anyone who did not scramble out of my reach. Someone stopped me—a hefty sailor caught me and pushed me away from the others. I landed painfully on the splintery deck.

I huddled there and wept, remembering my life with Kamaka. I did not want to see him, but the images came. I saw him scrambling up a tall tree and dropping breadfruit to me at the bottom. And diving from the highest rocks into a swimming hole! I saw him trapping a wild pig. And laughing. Kamaka was always laughing.

I banged my head on the ship's deck, hoping to send those memories away.

They went, but then I saw my mother hushing Kimi when she cried from a stubbed toe, plaiting *hala* leaves into sleeping mats, and competing with Lani to tell the funniest stories.

The memories made me cry even harder. Other people in the cattle hold were weeping too. We wailed the names of our families, our villages, and our beloved islands.

Some people cried out to God.

But praying did no good. The steamer did not turn around. It lurched steadily toward the leprosy prison on Moloka'i island. I did not expect God to be waiting there for us.

We were alone now. We would have to find our way without Him.

Even He could not cure our disease.

2

Ke Kahunapule
[THE PRIEST]

I have forgotten many things about my sun-filled days as a child in Honolulu. But certain events followed me here to Moloka'i, and suddenly, after I haven't thought of them for a very long time, a face, a pleasant smell, or a movement will place them in front of me.

The time the Catholic missionaries arrived is one of those days. It was the priest with spectacles who stayed in my mind. Something about his bewildered look and the way he pushed his glasses up on his nose made him stand out from all the others.

It was a carefree sunny day and I was riding horseback with Kamaka.

"Hurry, Pia!" he called. "A ship is coming in." He turned his horse *makai,* toward the sea.

I dug my heels into Māui's side and he picked up speed. Pele galloped ahead with Kamaka on her back. She turned as she neared the sea, and Māui followed. We galloped over wet sand, racing toward Honolulu's harbor.

I had almost caught up to Kamaka when I had to slow down. A crowd had gathered at the wharf. Vendors sold oranges and pineapples, flower garlands and woven hats. Horse traders and businessmen called out for buyers. Everyone was eager to earn a little silver.

Kamaka found a spot in the shade of a tree, and we watched from our horses. The sailing ship, the *R. W. Wood,* was from

Europe. Kamaka had sailor friends on this vessel and sometimes he helped them unload cargo.

Something good was sure to arrive—perhaps tools and colorful dry goods for the marketplace, or machines for the sugar mills, or books and slates for our schools. And pleasure seekers who would pay money for tours around our islands.

Children and grown-ups crowded close to get a good look at the new arrivals.

You should have seen how we always stared at foreigners with their formal habits and pale color. We imagined what their lands were like by seeing how they were dressed. And we begged them for stories of castles and cowboys.

Soon the ship came close enough for us to see who was on board. We could tell from their garments that they were missionaries.

"Catholics," said Kamaka.

European missionaries were often Catholics. America sent lots of Protestants, and sometimes Mormons. Kamaka didn't care much for any of those religions. He said he preferred Hawai'i's old gods. But truthfully, no one really believed in *them* anymore, not since long ago, when one of our kings broke a taboo—eating with women. Something terrible could have happened to him. But lightning did not strike, and Pele, our fire goddess, did not erupt from her home in the volcano. So the king pronounced our Hawaiian religion dead.

Then the Protestants from America arrived with a new God. That was in 1820. The teachers in our schools made sure we knew this date. They told us how Hawai'i eventually turned to the true God. That was because another of our kings declared Christianity our official religion.

After that, missionaries poured in like lava.

On this day, a stream of nuns in white robes came off the

ship first. They wobbled down the gangplank with the help of the ship's crew.

A row of children squatting in the dirt giggled at the Catholics coming off the boat. They laughed because the missionaries looked strange and were unsteady on their feet. And because they were excited to see what new things the foreigners brought this time.

"*Aloha* to you," the children sang in one voice. "*Aloha.*" They reached out to touch the nuns as they walked past.

And our grown-ups? They stuck their hands out to welcome the strangers. Every Hawaiian at the wharf wanted to shake hands with each of the missionaries.

There were ten nuns and then five priests. No, not five, but six. A straggler was talking to the sailor named Baldrik—Kamaka's friend. The priest glanced at his companions, who were headed toward the customs house. But he didn't follow them. He seemed determined to convince Baldrik of some important thing.

Baldrik shook his head and urged the priest to join his companions. Finally, when one of the other missionaries called to him, the priest left Baldrik standing there and bobbed his way down the plank. But he kept looking back toward the sailor, as if he hated to let him go.

The priest was stocky, with thick brown hair, and he wore spectacles that slipped down his nose. He paused, pushed the glasses up, and looked around him. He squinted to see us more clearly.

Someone dropped a garland of purple flowers around his neck, bumping into his spectacles so that he had to push them up again. A wrinkled old *tūtū* reached up to put a yellow *lei* on him.

Then the crowd pushed in. Everyone wanted to shake *his* hand also.

The priest seemed confused by all this *aloha,* but he greeted everyone who reached out to him. Soon my people surrounded him and I couldn't see him anymore.

The sailor named Baldrik came to Kamaka and said they needed him to move cargo.

I wanted to go, too, but Captain Geerken didn't like children underfoot. I was only eight years old. Kamaka was fifteen, strong and muscular.

Baldrik told us that during the voyage the missionaries had helped them work on the ship. "The stocky one named Damien worked as hard as any sailor," he said. "Did you see him just now, trying to save my soul? To him I am doomed because I'm not a Catholic."

"Baldrik," shouted Captain Geerken from the deck of the ship. "You're on duty."

Kamaka and Baldrik left me there. So I turned Māui and followed the crowd that walked alongside the new missionaries. They had turned onto Fort Street.

The Catholic church was full by the time I had tied Māui, so I stood outside the window and peered in. The new missionaries were filing in, but I could only see glimpses of them through the crowd. And the galleries above were filled with our people.

The Catholic religion was so powerful that even outside I could feel it all around me. I felt the warmth of candles and the thick smell of incense. A hymn spilled out the window. I could not understand the Latin words, but still I could hear the joy in it.

I wondered what islands the missionaries would move to. I knew that my Protestant teachers would be sure to warn me about them. They taught us that Catholics were idolaters because they worshiped images of Jesus and the Virgin Mother.

It was hard *not* to enjoy the beauties inside the Catholic church. To me, it seemed a happier church than the church of the Protestants. The Catholics seemed to smile more and their buildings were filled with color. And what Hawaiian doesn't like color?

But the service was in Latin. Who wants to listen to words they can't understand?

I turned and headed toward the harbor. I knew that these missionaries would scatter to various islands, and I would probably never see any one of those priests again.

3

Ka Hahai

[TO FOLLOW]

Several years after those priests arrived, I had another experience that is still as real to me as life on Moloka'i. It was much like any other day in Honolulu. The trade winds were gentle, the air was filled with the sweet scent of our flowering trees, and the mountains were rich with color.

By this time I was thirteen years old. I spent my days in school and endured all that the teachers asked of me. I composed a poem about Hawai'i and memorized the names of twelve European countries. I added and subtracted numbers and practiced reading and penmanship.

But my heart was with Kamaka. I knew he was leading some tourists on an expedition. He would be done by the time I was finished with lessons.

After class I dashed outside, climbed onto Māui, and rode to Kamaka's house. I found him napping on a mat outside his door. When my shadow crossed his face he jumped to his feet.

"Okay!" he said. "I thought you would never come!"

He picked up the bundle beside him and tied it onto his horse. Then he climbed onto Pele and prodded her into a run. Māui and I followed. We were off on a mountain adventure. We had planned it for days. My mother would not worry about me; after all, I was safe with Kamaka.

We rode *mauka*—toward the mountain—past the patches where *kalo* grew and up into the forest. I could almost feel the arithmetic and geography sliding off my back. I pulled off my shirt and stuffed it into one of my saddlebags. I threw my shoulders back and enjoyed the feel of the wind in my ears.

The forest was shadowy and cool. Tree ferns brushed our arms and yellow hibiscus blossoms hung down into our path. At first, sunlight made bright designs on the trail. But soon the trees were so crowded that no light came through at all.

We crossed a stream and then rode alongside it. The path grew steeper, and after a while we let our horses drink at a deep pool. I slid to the ground and put my face into the water, too. I loved the smell of moss and leaves and forest streams.

I should have known better than to put my face into the water before Kamaka put *his* face in. Suddenly I felt his foot on my backside. And the next thing I felt was cold on my head and then my shoulders. I tumbled into the deep pool of water.

I held my breath and let myself go.

When I came to the surface, I shook the water out of my eyes and looked around. I didn't see Kamaka anywhere. But I heard him laughing. And then I heard a tree limb shake overhead and a loud "Okay!" and felt a huge splash right beside me.

I waited until I saw Kamaka's curly black hair coming through the surface. He was smiling even before he came out of the water. Before he could take a good gulp of air I grabbed his head and pushed him down. Of course he pulled me with him. We battled each other until I begged him to leave me alone.

That's how our games always went. Kamaka was so fast and strong that he never got tired before I did.

We climbed back onto our horses and rode higher into the hills. Soon we were too high up for many trees or shrubs to grow. Ahead of us were gray lava peaks. I was glad Māui was sure-footed and unafraid because the trail took us right to the edge of the mountain. I felt weak when I looked down.

Sometimes I wanted to turn around, but Kamaka and Pele went first, and I knew that if they could do it, Māui and I could too. Ahead of us I saw more peaks. Many streams dropped from their sides into the depths. For nearly every waterfall there was a rainbow. The setting sun threw an orange glow onto the mountains, and in spite of my fear I wanted to stay in this place with Kamaka forever.

Finally we stopped. Kamaka climbed down and removed his large bundle from behind his saddle. He unrolled the leaf mats that covered it. Inside was fruit, a coconut, shrimps wrapped in a banana leaf, and a calabash of *poi*. And blankets.

We were very hungry by now, so we sat on one of the mats and put the calabash between us. I dipped my fingers into the thick, purplish paste and then into my mouth.

This *poi,* Hawai'i's favorite food, was as familiar to me as Kamaka himself. Together we had grown the *kalo* plants in a watery patch. And together we had harvested their fleshy corms. Kamaka had baked the tubers and I had helped him pound them, adding just the right amount of water.

After we ate, we opened the coconut and shared its milk. Then we cut the crisp white flesh into little pieces. We lay back on our mats and munched while Kamaka talked about the sightseers he'd led into the mountains that day.

"The woman was very brave," he said, "but her husband was like a child. I showed him four times how to make the horse jump across the gulch, but he would not do it. His wife did it without fear. And then she had to do it again because the man paid me extra to turn around. So I took them by the easy trail, and while we rode I told him about the Marchers of the Night."

I shivered and reached for one of the blankets Kamaka had brought.

"Did you scare him?" I asked. "What about the woman?"

"The woman thinks Hawai'i's spirits are silly. But still she's very curious about our legends. So I told her the Night Marchers are giants of men. I showed her how they chant and carry torches as they march to the sea."

"Did you tell her that your *tūtū* herself has seen them?"

"Of course," said Kamaka. "I told her they appear out of nowhere and every Hawaiian fears the thought of meeting them. I said that if a house is in their path they will march right through it. When I said that, the man begged me to stop. But his wife patted his hand and said, 'Now, dear, there is no truth in Hawai'i's legends.'"

Kamaka does not like it when foreigners deny our spirits. Mostly we have rejected them ourselves. But the Night Marchers— well, every Hawaiian knows someone who claims to have seen them. And lying out there in the forest that night I had to look around to convince myself they weren't nearby.

I pulled the blanket more tightly around me. "What would *you* do?" I asked Kamaka. "If the Night Marchers appeared to you?"

Of *course* fearless Kamaka did not hide beneath a blanket. He did not tremble or talk of running. He laughed and said boldly, "I would join them in their march." He slapped me on the shoulder. "You would join them too, Pia. You are braver than any foreigner."

But I didn't feel so brave right then. I was afraid I would dream of the Night Marchers. Was I safe there at the top of the mountain?

I stayed awake a long time after Kamaka's breathing told me he was asleep. Pele and Māui were sleeping too. I pulled my blanket around my shoulders, and it made me feel safer.

And besides, Kamaka was close by. There was nothing to be afraid of. Before long the Marchers of the Night seemed far away and not so real.

I rolled onto my tummy and was nearly asleep when I heard Kamaka talking. "Go away!"

"What?"

"Go away. I can't look at you."

I sat up. Had the Night Marchers come? I looked around, afraid that I would see torches coming over the precipice. But it was dark. And the only thing I heard was the sound of the wind. Then Kamaka called out again. Louder this time.

"No! I don't want to see you. Leave me alone." He squirmed wildly on his mat like a shrimp washed onto shore. And he sounded frightened. "Go away! Go away!"

I shook him then. "Kamaka. Wake up! They are not here. The Night Marchers are not here."

Kamaka shook himself as if he wanted to come awake. "What?" he asked. And then he realized I was there. He realized where he was.

"You were dreaming about the Marchers of the Night," I said. "You didn't want to look at them. But you're awake now and they're not here." It felt strange for me to say those things to him, as if Kamaka was a frightened child and I was the grown-up.

Kamaka got up and went to his saddlebag. He came back with two bananas and handed one to me. We were back to our old way now, with him taking care of me. He began to eat and I started asking questions.

"How did they look?" I asked. "Were they really big?"

"Who?"

"The Night Marchers. You were dreaming."

Kamaka laughed then and shook his head. "No," he said. "I did not dream about the Night Marchers."

So I asked him what he was dreaming about.

"Let's sleep," he said. He lay back on his mat and began to

sing a sailor song he'd learned from Baldrik. And the next thing I knew, the sun was peeking over the mountain range ahead of us.

Even with my eyes shut I knew that Kamaka was climbing out of his blankets, stretching his arms and legs, eager for a day of play. The morning was cool here on the mountain, so I snuggled into my mat and pulled the blanket over my head. I wasn't ready to greet the day.

But I couldn't lie there for long. Kamaka was ready for adventure. He pulled the blanket away from me and put his big toes nearly into my face. "Up with you, lazy one," he said.

I wanted to push his foot away and turn over. But I sat up instead. Kamaka handed me a mango fruit. Its cool, yellow sweetness brought me awake. The juice of it dripped down my chin and onto my chest. I shivered. He threw my shirt at me and I pulled it over my head.

Pele and Māui stamped impatiently. They were tired of standing at the top of this mountain.

While we rode, I kept my eye on Pele and Kamaka to see what was ahead. We traveled down and down, slipping at times, when loose rocks went tumbling into the depths.

I didn't like danger, but I would do anything Kamaka asked of me. Even when I was terrified I knew I could do it if he went first.

After a while Kamaka called back, "Waterhole ahead!"

I was glad of that. My muscles ached from hanging on to my horse during the steepest parts of the ride. I was thirsty and knew that our horses would be too.

But I found out that Māui and Pele would have to wait. When Kamaka stopped his horse and hopped off, there was no waterhole in sight. He stripped off his straw hat, his white shirt and blue trousers. I could see he had a swimming spot hidden away somewhere.

I followed him to a rock overhang and looked out over the edge. I saw a large pool of water below. It was farther than I had ever dived before. "How did you find this place?" I asked.

"I discovered it when I was leading some Americans on an expedition."

Kamaka poised himself at the edge of the rock. I looked again to the water far below. "Did you dive here before?"

"Of course." Kamaka leaned forward.

"Did they dive too?"

He stopped. "What?"

"The Americans. Did they dive here?"

"Oh, no. They were afraid." Kamaka took a deep breath and put his hands out wide. He started to lean forward again.

"How deep is the water down there?"

Kamaka stepped back and looked at me. "It's plenty deep. And wide enough, too. Are you scared?"

"Oh, no," I said. "If you can do it, I can do it."

"Of course," said Kamaka. "Now watch how I do it." He leaned forward, spread his arms, and dived straight and clean into the water below. Just watching him made me feel like I was falling, too. I grabbed for a small tree beside the rock I was standing on.

I waited for Kamaka to come up out of the water. It took a long time. But finally he came up. "Okay!" I heard him call. "Come on, Pia." He swam to the edge of the pool and waited.

I knew I had to go. But I had lied to Kamaka. I wanted to be as strong and fast and daring as he was. I *wanted* to do everything he could do, but I could not. I *was* afraid.

I heard him down there calling my name. I had to dive. I stood at the edge of the rock, in the same spot where Kamaka had stood. I breathed deeply. I leaned forward and felt the earth shake.

But I spread my arms and dived. "Okay!" The earth shook again, harder this time. All the way down I felt it shaking. I saw rocks and trees going up past me and the water coming at me. I moved my hands out ahead of me to break through the water. I felt the cold and knew that I had not broken my head open on a rock. I was going down into the depths.

I held my breath and let the good feeling bring me up.

And when I came to the top Kamaka was there. He grabbed me and shouted, "Bully for you, Pia! You were not afraid." He was so proud and I felt so pleased with myself that I did not tell him the truth. I let him think I was as brave as he was.

We swam then and looked up at the rock overhang and congratulated ourselves for being so daring. We did not play games or push each other into the water as we had the day before.

But then I decided to trick Kamaka. It would be my revenge on him for shoving me into the water when I was getting a drink. I swam to the other side of the waterhole and began to yell.

"Help me, Kamaka. My leg—it hurts. I cannot move it. Help! I'm drowning!"

With my mouth open, still calling for help, I slid slowly beneath the water. I went down and down and then when I thought Kamaka would be worrying I kicked my legs and pushed myself back up. When I came close to the top, I saw a face above the water. And a hand reaching out to me. I reached for the hand.

I would let Kamaka pull me onto the rocks and then I would jump up and laugh at the frightened look on his face. I would show him I was not hurt. It would be a good prank.

But before I could take the hand, I heard Kamaka's voice. "Don't touch him!" he said fiercely.

I felt Kamaka grab me from behind. I heard his soft grunts as he swam with me under his arm. I was confused. Someone else must have reached out to me. But who?

I looked back to see.

A man kneeling at the water's edge stared after us. Right away I could see the leprosy tumors that covered his face. That's why Kamaka was dragging me away!

The disease of leprosy was spreading across Hawai'i's islands. My mother's sister had had it. And now, seeing that man's face, I remembered my aunt's death.

Kamaka urged me to the other side of the water and we crawled onto a rock. I looked back for the man with leprosy, but he had disappeared into the forest.

"Don't stare!" said Kamaka as if he thought I would catch the disease by just looking at it.

"That man," I panted. "He had leprosy."

Suddenly Kamaka was as serious as a missionary. His dark eyes blazed and he gripped my arm. He narrowed his eyes into little slits and set his brown jaw in a hard line. "That man must be hiding in the mountains so the authorities won't ship him to Moloka'i."

"Moloka'i! I've heard that if you go to Moloka'i you can't come back again. That man should die at home with his family! Kamaka, we should help him!"

"No!" Kamaka nearly shouted when he said it, and his voice sounded the way it had during the night when he was dreaming. Almost like he was frightened.

I knew that the foreigners were afraid of leprosy. But most of our people were not.

"Our king has to protect the rest of us," said Kamaka. "If they don't go away, their disease will kill us all. Leprosy is contagious. You don't want to get it, do you?"

Kamaka was right. I did not want to get leprosy. What would happen to me if I did? I shuddered just thinking about being sent away to Moloka'i.

But Kamaka steadied me with his strong arm. "Don't worry, Pia," he said. "I will protect you."

Of course it was true. Kamaka had always protected me. Still, in spite of his promise, I felt for a moment like the earth was shaking.

4

Ka ʻOhana

[FAMILY]

Many times while scrounging for food here on Molokaʻi I have been tortured with memories of a certain *lūʻau* back home on Oʻahu. The feast was to celebrate the birthday of a baby in the village.

Everyone passed the baby around and admired his round face and fat legs. A young woman handed him to Kamaka. He removed a *lei* of pink orchids from his straw hat and draped it over the naked boy. Then Kamaka lifted the baby above his head. "See the child!" he said. "May he run like Māui, the fastest and most clever of Hawaiʻi's heroes!"

Everyone around us cheered.

Kamaka was twenty years old then and I was thirteen. I was still trying to keep up with him, but it seemed that lately his eyes were always on women. And I was more interested in our old adventures.

Soon he would probably marry. Then he would have even less time for me. Sometimes it seemed to me I was losing him already.

I watched a few of the men lifting the steaming banana leaves from the ground oven. Then they removed the cooked pig, and I realized I could not wait to eat. I sat on a mat and Kamaka sat beside me.

Other families unrolled their mats and joined us. Women distributed *kī* leaves with slices of yellow fruit. The men brought large calabash bowls of *poi* they'd pounded from *kalo* roots.

As I dipped my finger into the *poi*, I heard my name. I turned to see my mother, standing behind me. She nestled the baby in her arms. Her eyes were bright with happiness because she loved babies.

"Pia," she said. "You were smaller even than this the first time you saw Kamaka."

I had heard this story many times, but I stopped eating and listened again because it was the story of important beginnings.

My little sister crowded into the circle and settled herself beside me. Kimi was so tiny and she wanted to be near me. I put my arm around her and together we listened to our mother's story.

"Kamaka was seven years old when you were born," my mother said to me. "He was out playing with the lizards, and Lani dragged him in to see you."

Kamaka's mother elbowed mine and leaned in to speak.

"You should have heard Kamaka protest," she said. "He dragged his heels in the dust and shouted that I made him lose his lizard in the bushes. He had seen babies before, but he had not seen this lizard. Tūtū had to help me drag him inside. We plopped him there in front of you and told him to greet you. Kamaka crossed his arms in defiance and growled, '*Aloha* to you, Pia.'"

Everyone laughed and my mother picked up the story. "You opened your sleepy eyes and saw that big boy, and you've been following him around ever since!"

I laughed with proud embarrassment. I had eaten my first *poi* from Kamaka's finger. He had caught lizards for me, carried me on his back, and taught me to ride horses. When I thought about those things—the ways Kamaka had been almost a father to me—I knew that I would never really lose him.

After all, hadn't he been there from the beginning?

5

Ka Maʻi Pākē

[THE CHINESE SICKNESS—LEPROSY]

Then, one morning, everything about my life changed.

It started like any other day with Yellow Cat jumping on my face. I yawned and pulled him onto my shoulder. I scratched his cheek and waited for his purring to put me back to sleep.

I felt my mother shaking me. "Wake up, Pia, you have school today."

I opened one eye.

Sunlight streamed through the door. Parrots chattered in the palm trees outside. I groaned and turned over on my mat. What illness would convince my mother to let me stay home? "Maybe I'll tell her my throat hurts," I whispered to Yellow Cat.

I lay there dreaming of how I could spend the day with Kamaka, working in the *kalo* patch or swimming at Waikīkī. I imagined myself swimming faster than he could. But then I heard them again—the purr of Yellow Cat and the voice of my mother.

"Pia! Don't make me call you again. You have school today, and no sickness you can dream up will keep you home." My mother pulled my blanket off.

"Pia!" she gasped. "What—what have you done to yourself?" Her voice cracked. "Oh, not *you*, Pia, not my only son."

Suddenly I was fully awake. I sat up.

"Lie down," she commanded. She pushed me back onto my tummy. "Your shoulder. There are spots."

I lay there while she examined my neck and shoulders. *I*

probably slept with a mosquito, I thought. *If only mosquito bites could keep me out of school …*

"*Auē!*" my mother moaned. "This is so terrible. *Auē!*" She slumped onto the mat beside me. She fell across my body and squeezed me so hard I hurt. Her hot breath warmed my back and I felt her tears washing over my shoulder blades.

I shuddered without even knowing why.

"What?" I demanded. "What is wrong?" I tried to raise myself. I wanted to see what my mother was so worried about. But the weight of her body pressed me to my mat.

"You cannot go to school," she said. "Your teachers might see them."

I tried again to sit up, and this time she let me push her away. I strained to see the spots, but it was impossible. "*I* can't even see them," I said. "How could my teachers find them?"

"You could get new spots on your forehead or your elbows." My mother pulled at her hair and moaned.

My sister stared. Her large brown eyes were wider than ever. Slowly her thin face crumpled and she began to wail. "*Auē, auē …*"

"You'd think I was dying!" I shouted. "Why do you cry as if you were at my burial?"

Suddenly I wanted desperately to go to school. I couldn't wait to take the examination my teacher had planned. I jumped to my feet and pulled on my pants. I ran my fingers through my hair and began putting on my shirt. But I was nervous and had trouble with the buttons.

My mother interfered, pulling me hard against her. "You cannot go," she said. "You have—you have—" She was sobbing. "Lep—lep—leprosy." Her voice shook so that I barely understood her. "The spots, they are just like my sister's. The teachers will find out and then they will ship you away."

She is teasing me, I told myself. *I don't feel sick. She knows I was going to pretend to be ill, so she's trying to scare me into school.*

I knew it wasn't true. My mother loved to tease, but she wouldn't play with me about such a dreadful thing. And since I couldn't believe such unbearable news, I taunted her. "At least you won't have to drag me out of bed every day." My voice went into the soft darkness of her clothing.

She thrust me away from her then, so hard that I fell back on my mat. "I am not playing with you!" she screamed. "You have leprosy. I know it when I see it. And there is nothing good about the leprosy island. There is not enough shelter there and never enough food." Her voice slipped and rose in a terrible chanting. "And no eating *poi* with your family, no Yellow Cat, and no Kamaka …"

Her terror spilled onto me then. It burned my insides until my legs felt like the tentacles of a jellyfish. I needed to run.

Kimi wailed, and my fear grew hotter. I had to escape! I crawled past the two of them and out the door. But they followed me to the doorway. My mother slumped against the door-frame crying, "*Auē, auē,* Pia."

I jumped to my feet then and ran to my horse. I slipped the rope from the fence post and grabbed Māui's black mane, pulling myself onto his back. I dug in my heels and slapped him into a gallop.

But I could not outrun Kamaka's voice. *Leprosy is contagious,* he had said on that day in the mountains.

I didn't know if leprosy was contagious. I only knew that the foreigners thought it was, and for some reason Kamaka believed them.

I hadn't touched the sick man in the mountains, had I? No, I was sure I had not. Kamaka had been there to protect me. Then how did I get the disease?

34

The face of my mother's sister floated into my mind. She had died at her house before the government began sending people with leprosy away. She'd lived a long time at home. Eventually she'd lost the feeling in her fingers. I'd seen her holding the hot rocks of the ground oven while digging out baked sweet potatoes. She did not flinch when the heat of the rocks sizzled her flesh.

"At least it doesn't hurt," I said to Māui. "At least leprosy doesn't feel bad." But as soon as I said it, I remembered my aunt's death. I heard again her moaning for water. I saw the swollen mouth she could no longer close.

"Go!" I screamed to Māui. "Faster!" I leaned into the wind and urged my horse to outrun the memories. "Take me to a place where leprosy cannot go," I pleaded.

Maybe I should head him into the sea, I thought. That would put an end to the leprosy. I could die quickly and Kamaka would be glad that I didn't have to go to Moloka'i.

Kamaka. When I imagined him finding me dead, I nearly cried for the grief he would feel.

Kamaka had always been the one to repair my wounds, cleaning the dirt from a stubbed toe or pressing crushed *noni* leaves onto a cut on my heel. He'd taught me everything I knew about Hawai'i's plants—the ones to use for healing, and how to plant crops for food. Together we had waded through the watery *kalo* patch, harvesting tubers like father and son.

I had never known who my real father was. I only knew that he was *haole*, a white foreigner. Even if my mother's looking glass had not told me this truth, there were plenty of people around me who had. For as long as I could remember, I'd been called *hapa haole*, half-white.

I supposed my father was a sailor who'd come and gone when it pleased him. But whenever I asked her, my mother frowned and pushed my question aside. "Don't worry about him," she would say. "He isn't here. But Kamaka is. Be glad you have Kamaka."

I *was* glad. And now, suddenly, I knew I must find him. He would know some remedy. Kamaka would make everything right. I turned my horse toward home.

By the time I tied Māui to the fencepost, the sun was high in the sky. My family wasn't home. The yard was silent except for the clacking of palm branches in the breeze and the clucking of chickens as they searched for worms under the sugarcane. I brought a knife from the cookhouse and cut a stalk of the cane. With a sharp whack I cut a section for chewing. Then I cut shorter lengths to give my sister when she returned.

I sat in the red dirt under a banana tree and nibbled on the cane. My aloneness moved in on me like a dense fog. I didn't know where my mother was. Probably at Kamaka's home, crying with Lani and Tūtū. She had heard too many stories about Moloka'i.

Some Hawaiians said the stories couldn't be true. Lani insisted that the Board of Health would not dump our people on a desolate peninsula without enough food and clothing. And if they did have needs, they would share with each other.

"After all," she'd say, "they *are* Hawaiians."

"I hope the rumors are exaggerated," my mother would say.

But other people believed the rumors. Some angry citizens wrote letters to the newspapers. They said it was unfair to separate sick people from their families just when they needed them most. On cool evenings, after sharing a meal of fish and *poi,* my mother had read these letters to Lani and Tūtū.

"I'm glad the settlement was not there when my sister had leprosy," my mother would say. "At least when she died, she was at home with her family."

Kamaka agreed with his mother that the sick people on

Moloka'i could help one another. "They can be 'ohana to each other, just as we are like family," he said. "It's better for everyone that they go."

But mostly Kamaka didn't like to think about such sad things. "Come," he would say to me whenever the subject of leprosy came up. "Let's go for a swim." And while the women argued over what happened to people with leprosy, we would escape to the adventures of the sea.

I hadn't thought much about it until after the day when the man with leprosy had tried to help me in the water. On that day Kamaka's laughing eyes had become dark points of fear.

No, it couldn't be fear. Kamaka was fearless.

Wasn't he?

I sat alone in our yard and wondered what Kamaka would do when he found out.

How can I tell him? Why did I think he could fix it? Slowly, as these questions pressed in on me, the sweet juice of the sugarcane turned sour in my mouth.

The cane slipped from my fingers onto the red earth. Ants scurried to devour it. My mother's crying echoed deep within me and I put my head between my knees and started to moan.

The chickens settled into the dust at my feet. Suddenly the day was hot and desolate. In the awful stillness I began to feel how it would be to live the rest of my life without the things I loved.

I cried then—for Kimi and the way it felt to carry her on my back. I cried for Hawai'i's soft nights with family swapping gossip around a fire. For the bright eyes I saw through the flames. And for the stories and laughter that swirled around us like sweet-smelling smoke in the darkness.

I grieved because I hadn't learned to swim as fast as Kamaka. And now it was too late.

Hurry, Kamaka. Come. There isn't much time.

6

Ke Kali ʻAna

[WAITING]

For weeks I sat on a wooden bench in the enclosed yard at the Kalihi Hospital. Every morning I saw my shadow shrinking and every afternoon I watched it grow long again. I had nothing to do but sit and wait for Kamaka.

I waited when school was not in session, when I should have been surf-riding and fishing. I waited on days when other children were in school. For the first time, I wished *I* could be in class. I wanted to read and write and cipher. I wanted to think of something besides losing my family. And Kamaka.

My despair over Kamaka was like my shadow—shrinking in the brightness of each new day and growing again as the day passed.

I didn't know how long I would be in this leprosy hospital or when the Board of Health would send me to Molokaʻi. Most days I wanted to stay on Oʻahu forever. But after clutching the bars of Kalihi's high wooden fence for weeks, straining for the sight of Kamaka, I almost wished to be sent away. At least on Molokaʻi I would not torture myself with false hope.

Only my mother and Kimi visited, bringing newspapers to pass the time and pineapple or sugarcane to sweeten my imprisonment. But my mother could never be cheerful for long. Soon she would pound the fence that separated us.

"My son, my son," she would moan. "Is this the last time I will see you?"

One day, during my fourth week at the hospital, she seemed more angry than sad. "Stop looking for Kamaka," she said. "The man hasn't dipped two fingers into our *poi* since the day he heard about your leprosy. He doesn't come around anymore, and his own mother doesn't know where he's hiding."

Kamaka hiding? Magnificent and invincible Kamaka who is afraid of nothing? "Hiding from what?"

"He is ashamed," said my mother. "And he should be—for deserting you like this. Lani thinks he went to Puna."

Puna? The home of Kīlauea, the great volcano? Kamaka was supposed to take me there. The two of us had planned to visit Pele, the goddess of fire on the island of Hawai'i. For two years we'd dreamed of climbing to the rim of her crater. We imagined our proud faces gleaming in her hot, liquid glow. It would not matter if she scorched our flesh and sent us down the mountain with her sulfur fumes. We would laugh with the thrill of being young and invincible.

By now, I knew that only Kamaka was invincible. *I* had been conquered already—by leprosy. Just yesterday I had felt a small lump forming below my ear.

"Come, Kamaka," I whispered into the darkness that night. "I can escape this hospital and we can run to the mountains together. We will hide from the sheriff when he rounds up people with leprosy to ship them to Moloka'i. You know the mountains, Kamaka. And I have proved I can live in them also. Please come."

I prayed that God would send Kamaka to me. I prayed that I would not have leprosy after all. And that the officials would not send me to Moloka'i.

But nothing changed. God was not listening.

In the early days at the hospital, I had been hopeful. Each time the foreign doctors examined me, I convinced myself I did not have the dreaded leprosy. But the days slipped by and then the weeks. With each inspection by the doctors, with each sad shake of their heads, I could feel hope sliding away like the sun slipping over Honolulu's harbor.

Like my belief that God was listening to my prayers.

Then on a listless afternoon, about six months after I came to the hospital, an attendant interrupted my nap in the courtyard. "Wake up, Pia. You have a visitor."

A visitor? It couldn't be my mother. She'd been there earlier in the day. Maybe it was Kamaka. I almost ran to see who had come.

A large woman—sad and as familiar as family—stood there waiting for me. It was Kamaka's *tūtū*.

"Pia, oh, Pia, is it you?" Tūtū began to weep the moment she saw me. She reached for me and then realized she could not gather me into her arms. So she sagged against the fence that separated us. She covered her face with her hands, and her tears ran like rivers down her fleshy arms. They dripped off her dimpled elbows and splashed onto the wooden floor.

I waited, heavy with guilt for causing such unhappiness.

After a while Tūtū's tears lessened, but still she did not speak. She lowered herself onto the bench behind her. She reached helplessly from time to time and opened her mouth as though to talk. But Tūtū, giver of hugs and playful swats on the bottom, could not speak without touching me. And touching she was not supposed to do.

So she looked at me and did not say a word. I traced a crack in the floor with my big toe and thought it odd that I couldn't feel the place where the two boards met. I shifted in my seat and waited for Tūtū to speak. I wanted to help her and thought I should speak first. But I didn't know what to say.

Tūtū shifted her large body on the bench and shoved her

hands under her heavy thighs. She opened and closed her mouth several times and then she stuttered, "Are—are—are they taking good care of you, Pia? Is the *poi* fresh?"

I nodded even though I couldn't remember what I had eaten since coming to the hospital.

"I am ashamed for Kamaka," said Tūtū.

"I hear he went to Hawai'i."

Tūtū shook her head. "Maybe," she said. "But yesterday he came back for a hug from his old grandmother. He clung to me like a barnacle on a whaling ship. But my hugs didn't make him feel better. He is not the old fun-loving Kamaka."

"Is he coming to see me?"

Tūtū shook her head.

"But why?"

I thought of how I had been willing to climb every mountain Kamaka had taken me to. There was no volcano I would not explore with him. No distance I would not dive for him. How had I failed?

"He is afraid," said Tūtū.

"Afraid? Of what?"

Tūtū shook her head and a new sadness crossed her face. "Kamaka was once a child, too," she said. Her voice faded into a whisper, and she seemed far away from me then—as if she'd gone back to that time when Kamaka was a boy.

Of course I knew Kamaka had been a child. But to me, he'd always seemed so fearless. I wanted to hear what Tūtū was remembering, but she could not make herself speak. And I did not have the courage to drag the story from her.

While I sat there trying to imagine Kamaka's fears, the attendant returned. "Are you Pia's *tūtū*?" she asked.

Tūtū began to weep again.

"A notice has been sent to the family," the attendant said. "Pia will leave tomorrow. In the evening a steamer will give him passage to Moloka'i. Send food and clothing with him. He will need it."

Tūtū began to wail. The sound of it followed me as I went down the hallway.

I saw the sun coming through the windows of the hospital. I saw the wooden floor where the golden beams shone. I stepped on each bright space. But I did not feel the sun's warmth. I did not feel any part of the floor where I walked. No part of me felt anything on that walk away from Tūtū.

Tomorrow a steamer would take me from home and family to the leprosy settlement on Moloka'i. I would be banished forever to the living grave. Everyone said it was the same as being dead already. Perhaps that was why I didn't feel anything.

7

ʻAʻole Kānāwai Ma Kēia Wahi

[IN THIS PLACE THERE IS NO LAW]

I stared at the leprosy peninsula. *This*, according to the Board of Health, was my new home.

The sight of it, along with the rocking of the steamer, made me want to vomit over the ship's rail. I took in large gulps of air so that I would not throw up. Others had been sick on this trip. I'd heard them during the night. But I was not one of *them*. Although the doctors said I had leprosy, I did not feel sick until I saw this place—a barren land edged with black rocks and rough seas. On the back side was a tremendous *pali*. The tops of those cliffs were covered with swirling clouds, so I could not tell how high they were. But it was obvious that they were taller than any *pali* I'd ever seen before.

So the rumors are true, I thought. *The high pali is a prison wall to keep us from escaping.*

Escape—why should they use that word to talk about sick people? We were not criminals! What had we done to deserve imprisonment?

As I stared at the cliffs I thought maybe it was not too late to escape. Maybe I could dive into the water when the sailors weren't looking. Or could I hide below in one of the berths?

But it *was* too late. The sailors were urging us down a rope ladder attached to the steamer rail. Below us, in the water, whaleboats waited to take us to shore. I decided I would let all the others go first. While they went, one of the sailors offered himself as my tour guide.

He pointed toward the far side of the peninsula. "There's a village way over there," he said. "Kalaupapa. Those people refused to leave their houses. So the government didn't force them to. But don't try to settle there. *Your* home is in Kalawao." The sailor gestured toward a spot that was inland a little way.

I thought I saw some rooftops, but the village of Kalawao was not easy to see from the ship. Closer to us was a black rock embankment at the edge of the sea, and beyond that a brown plain with boulders lying about.

"The hill behind the settlement is Kauhakō," said the sailor. "It's an old volcano."

I wondered if I could find shelter in the volcano's crater. But as if he knew my thoughts, the sailor dismissed that idea. "The crater is filled with water," he said. "They call it the given grave."

Had he said *grave*? I needed a place to live. And he was talking to me about dying?

Then another sailor urged me to leave the steamer. "Go on, boy! You can't live on this ship forever!"

I knew I had no choice. So I dropped my bundle into the whaleboat below. Then I crawled over the rail and climbed down the rope ladder. A cold wind jerked at it so that I almost lost my grip. Such a dangerous way to unload passengers! Couldn't they build a decent wharf?

Or weren't we worth the trouble?

Somehow I hung on until I reached the whaleboat. I settled myself inside and looked around. There were two sailors and three other patients.

One of the patients was a man with tears running down the creases in his cheeks. Another was a boy who was a little younger than I. Leprosy had made a straight row of lumps across his wide cheeks and down under his ears. His eyes were dark and narrow but they looked all around as if he did not want to miss a thing.

I hadn't noticed him before. But he remembered *me* and the way I'd kicked and screamed at everyone on board the steamer. He pulled himself as far from me as possible. "Stay away from *that* one," he said to the third patient in the boat. "He is not good."

The little girl stared at me, but she did not move away as the boy instructed. Her large eyes were like Kimi's—shy but trusting.

"*Aloha* to you," the boy said to her. "My name is Ah Loy. What is your name?"

The girl put two fingers into her mouth and did not answer.

Ah Loy turned to the man then. "*Aloha* to you. My name is Ah Loy. What is yours?"

The man stared off into the ocean. "My name is Hulu." I could barely hear him above the sound of the water lapping at the boat.

Ah Loy was not satisfied to know the man's name. "And where do you come from?" he asked.

"I have lived for all my life in Waipi'o," said Hulu. He spoke slowly and I could feel his sadness. "My wife is there. And my children, too. Even my children's children live in that valley. I will never see any of them again."

"True," said Ah Loy. "But we go to Moloka'i together. This is good. We are friends." Then he waved his hand at me. "But *he* is rude. He is *not* our friend."

Good, I thought. *I don't need friends. Does he think going to Moloka'i together will make it sweet?*

But one of the sailors seemed to agree with Ah Loy. "The boy is right," he said. "You should all stay together. You will have to be each other's family now."

Suddenly the little girl began to sob. She hunched her thin body over the woolen bundle she'd brought with her.

"She cries for her father," announced Ah Loy. "He wanted to be her *kōkua*. But he could not come to help her because he has other children. So he told her to find a *tūtū* to care for her."

"Ah," said the sailor. "The father gives good advice." He leaned forward to capture the girl's attention. "Tell me. What's in your parcel? A comb? Some soap? Whatever it is, just show it to some *tūtū* at the landing place and she'll take you straight home with her. You've got something she needs in that bundle. On Moloka'i they're desperate for everything. And *she's* got something for *you*—a house and protection. Hear me, girl?" He wagged his finger playfully. "Grab onto the *tūtū's* leg and don't let go."

He went back to rowing and the girl continued her sobbing. The quiet man reached out to pat her shoulder, but he seemed far away, probably back at home with his wife and his own little grandchildren.

I thought how wrong it was to send this child here without mother or father. She seemed so small, and her teeth clattered with the cold—or maybe it was fear that made her shake so. I didn't know if I could help, but I scooted closer. I thought she might shrink away from me because of what Ah Loy had said. But instead she leaned into me. And when she did the wind seemed less cold.

That's when I realized Ah Loy was right. It did feel better to go to the leprosy settlement with a friend.

But still, I was not ready for the moment when the boat brought us to the shore. Suddenly the deep blue changed to a churning whiteness where the waves broke. One of the sailors slipped over the side of the boat and struggled to gain his footing. The other sailor used the oars to steady us as much as possible.

Ahead, I saw patients from other whaleboats climbing onto the rocks. Water streamed from their clothing.

A few stray parcels floated in the sea and desperate patients tried to retrieve them.

I clutched my own bundle. I knew I could not lose it. It had my change of clothes, ointment for my sores, matches, and some food—everything I would need until my mother could send more.

The sailor who'd climbed into the water wanted to help the little girl out of the boat. He reached for her bundle, but she screamed and wouldn't let go. She leaned toward me. It made me think she wanted me to hold on to her, to keep her in the boat.

I wanted to. I wanted to take the oars and row both of us back to the ship. But the sailor reached for her bundle again. He yelled above the roar of the waves, "I'll give it back!"

The girl would not release her things, so he scooped *her* up, too, and called for someone on the rocks to help him. A large man with oily hair climbed down and took the girl from the sailor.

"You're next!" yelled the sailor, looking at me.

I didn't want to go, but I knew it didn't matter what I wanted. So I scrambled over the side of the boat, gripped my possessions, and rode the waves. When I saw a boulder waiting to smash me, I shoved my bundle between it and my head. The water slammed me against it and I bounced back, tossed like seaweed.

I reached my feet into the sand.

But there wasn't much sand. Rocks covered the floor of the landing place. Unable to get a foothold, I grabbed for a boulder. I hung on to it while I caught my breath. The waves battered me and I felt my hand slipping.

I thought of Kamaka then, of how he would coax me up treacherous mountain trails. I didn't want to think of him, and yet those memories helped me to hang on. I dragged myself over the rocky beach and climbed the black rocks that rose just above the shore. Then I stopped at the top to take in big gulps of air—and to see what I had come to.

Just ahead, I saw the little girl. The man still held her, but she was flailing her legs and pounding his chest with her fists. Then an old woman took pity on the girl and reached for her.

But he did not let go. "She's mine, Keona. I got her out of the water."

"No, Albert!" said the woman. "You have a house full of girls. This one is too young for you. Take your hands off her."

The child screamed and reached for the woman named Keona. "Tūtū!" she cried. "I want my *tūtū*."

The old woman smiled. "Albert, she won't let you sleep! She'll be crying for *tūtū* every day and all night."

Albert set the girl free then, as if he were scared of a crying child. But his eyes followed her in a way that made me feel he hadn't let her go. I could see he would not be a good father. He cared more for his own desires than he did for any small child.

When the girl slid out of Albert's arms she grabbed Keona's leg. Even when the old woman tried to pick her up, she would not let go.

Albert tucked in his shirttails and straightened his cravat. Then he looked toward the boat as if it might provide him with another girl.

I did not like the look of Albert. A heavy mustache drooped around the sides of his mouth, and loose skin puffed into dark bags beneath his small black eyes.

I was so busy watching him that I forgot to guard my bundle. But then I felt it slipping from my hand.

I turned to see a wicked grin on the face of the man who had taken it. "In this place there is no law," he announced, winking at someone who stood behind me.

I lunged for my bundle, but he was quick and shuffled it behind him, where another man latched onto it.

I tore at the second man and knocked him backward. I grabbed my bundle and started to run, but then I felt a hand on my shoulder. I turned and a tall, skinny man with only one bushy black eyebrow thrust his face into mine. "*Aloha* to you," he said. "My name is Boki. Stay with me and you'll be safe."

I looked at Boki and then at the other residents who had come to greet us. Boki seemed different somehow; it took me a moment to realize why.

Most of the people here wore clothing that was torn and layered with mud. But Boki's black pants and blue shirt were in good condition. And clean, too. His hair was trimmed and combed. He and Albert looked as if they belonged in Honolulu with vendors selling trinkets. Or providing women and rum to thirsty whalers.

I saw the two of them nodding and winking, using some secret language that the rest of us could not understand.

Beyond the people who came to watch us I could barely see their wooden houses. Between here and there were grass and rocks. Lots of rocks! And no trees.

Was this Hawai'i? Had they truly brought us to one of our islands? Where was the color?

I was used to green leafiness that spilled out of the mountains and down to the shore. And flowers of every color dripping from vines that covered trees, rock walls, and even our porches.

Boki must have seen me eyeing the settlement. "Every house is taken," he said. He gripped my shoulder. "But I will put a roof over your head."

Why did this man think I needed his roof? I knew how to build a dry shelter with sticks and thatches of grass.

"You'll starve without me," Boki warned.

But I didn't believe him. Kamaka had taught me everything he knew about the plants of Hawai'i and the foods they offered. And I could catch shrimps from the ocean.

Boki's hand tightened until I felt pain. "At my house you will have a man of power to protect you. That's hard to find in Kalawao."

I thought of the thieves who had tried to take my bundle. I could feel them watching me now, waiting for me to relax my grip. I wondered if Boki was working with them. Was he trying to distract me so they could catch me unawares?

I looked at Boki. He held himself proudly, as if he owned this place. Already I could feel his power.

But I also saw that he was blind in one eye.

That was when I knew for sure that I couldn't trust him. My mother had taught me that a one-eyed man meant bad luck.

I didn't need his protection. After all, I was not like the little girl who needed a father to care for her. I could look out for myself.

With a sudden twist I slipped out of Boki's hold and dashed away from this band of thieves.

8

Ka Hohono

[BAD-SMELLING]

My large bundle bounced awkwardly as I ran. But I was determined not to lose it—my only piece of home, my one link with survival.

I heard footsteps following me, and then a raspy voice. "Stop, boy! Come back!"

But I heard another voice inside me, and it pushed me on. *Run, Pia. You must learn to be fast!*

Even here, Kamaka's voice would not leave me.

I looked over my shoulder to see who was chasing me, and when I did, I tripped. By the time I was on my feet again, I heard him panting behind me.

"Stop!" he called again. His voice seemed to be right in my ear. I darted back and forth, dodging large rocks and hoping to wear him down. I too was getting tired, but I was determined not to let this man steal from me.

I thought maybe the panting sounds weren't so close now. But the man called out again. "Stop! The *luna* said stop!"

I wasn't falling for that trick! I kept on running. I didn't dare look back again for fear of stumbling.

Finally, I no longer heard footsteps. Only then did I turn to see if the man had given up.

He stood there in the rocky field shaking his head. I stopped and sagged against one of the large boulders to catch my breath. He shrugged, then turned away from me.

It hurt to breathe, so I tried only to think about that man plodding back toward the landing place. He was short—too short to be Boki. That meant someone *else* was trying to rob me.

I decided then to keep away from everyone. I couldn't understand what was happening in this place. Where was the *aloha*, Hawai'i's gentle, generous soul? Had it died when it reached these blackened shores?

It was so cold here. I searched for the sun but saw only the wooded cliffs looming behind me. Light and warmth would have a hard time finding their way into the leprosy settlement.

The village was just ahead now, so I decided to go and see what it was like.

I reached a muddy road lined with black boulders. On either side were clapboard houses with glass windows, and small porches on front and back. Most were enclosed with loosely stacked rock walls to discourage intruders. Beside one house I saw a few *kalo* plants, a patch of peas, and some sweet potato vines. But the yellowed leaves made me think the owner would not get much food from his garden.

On the *makai* side of the road was a picket fence surrounding a group of buildings, and a corral with some cows and a few horses. Dogs barked at me as I walked past. I heard a rooster crow.

For a moment I thought it could be any village in Hawai'i. It could be *my* village. But it wasn't. There were no flowers. No color at all, really. Just dirty white houses with peeling paint. And the gray and brown of rock walls with a few vines struggling over them. And only one tree.

The *hala* tree was so small and unimpressive that I almost hadn't seen it, standing by itself at the edge of the field of rocks. The shade it provided was so scarce that no one had even bothered to build a house beside it.

In spite of what the sailor had told me I headed toward the old volcano beyond the village. There were some trees growing on its slopes; perhaps I could find shelter there.

But I soon realized that others had built their homes among those trees. Thatched huts and crude shelters were scattered around the hill.

In the distance, at the western side of the peninsula, I saw the brightness of sunshine playing on the tops of trees. I longed to go there, but the sailor had said I was not allowed. And besides, I couldn't risk meeting anyone who might take my possessions.

So I turned toward the area behind the crater. The *pali* loomed over most of the peninsula, but here, near the crater, there was also a wooded valley that interrupted the cliffs. Surely I could find a cave there, a place where I could hide until Boki and everyone else stopped wanting something from me.

I climbed with my bundle over a rock wall and began my search.

I passed a lean-to made of sticks propped against a stone wall. As far as I could tell, no one was in it. But a tattered mat protruding from one end suggested that it was someone's home. I didn't want it anyway; I could build a better house.

When I reached the valley the sounds of the forest welcomed me. It was cooler there, and darker, too, but I cared only that others could not see me through the tangle of twisted branches and giant ferns.

I heard a noise and stopped to listen. It sounded like the snorting of a wild pig.

I considered what I should do. It would be best to go around him. Kamaka had taught me to trap and kill pigs, but I didn't want to startle one. A wild boar could be dangerous.

Before I could sneak away I saw it. He seemed to be feeding in a shallow ditch. A rumbling in my stomach reminded me that

I had not eaten since leaving Honolulu. What food did this pig have? I moved stealthily toward him to find out. Was it an edible root of some sort?

The pig was so engrossed in his meal that he did not seem to notice me. Still, I kept my distance while I peered through a snarl of twisted branches.

His meal appeared to be wrapped in an old blanket.

The boar grunted with pleasure as he ate. Certainly he was not eating roots. I leaned forward, squinting in the half darkness, until I recognized the shape of a ...

Surely not. But it was!

The pig dragged his meal a short distance and then a slant of light came in through the treetops. I could see it all more clearly now. He was feeding in a shallow grave. But whose?

And then I knew. It must be the grave of a leprosy patient. Like me.

The scene with the pig wobbled before my eyes. I grabbed a tree to steady myself. Surely I had not come to Moloka'i for this—to become food for pigs?

I forgot then about keeping out of the boar's way. I forgot about protecting my bundle. I threw it at the pig but it fell short, landing at the base of a large, moss-covered rock. I reached for stones on the forest floor. I hurled them at the pig. "Stop!" I screamed. "I'll kill you! I'll kill you!"

The startled pig stopped eating, looked at me, and charged.

I scrambled behind a boulder, but he came after me.

Once again I was being chased. And the pig could move more easily through the underbrush than I could. I picked up a rock and turned to face him. He was close and coming right at me.

I threw the rock and it hit him hard on the nose. He squealed and I threw another one. Then he turned to run. I watched as he hurtled into the underbrush, and then I ran, too—deep into the woods.

I ran until my legs crumpled beneath me. I huddled there with my knees and my forehead pressed to the earth of Moloka'i. It was damp and soft and smelled of decaying leaves. I vomited until my stomach was empty and the earth beneath me was foul.

9

Pohō Ka Manaʻolona
[DESPAIR]

The sour smell of my own vomit chased me through my dreams. Just when I thought I'd escaped it, the bad smell caught up to me.

I crisscrossed the peninsula looking for the village of healthy people. Instead, I found the old volcano and saw the watery grave at its bottom. I teetered there at its rim, trying to keep my balance. But suddenly I was falling—down and down into the darkness.

Fear shook me awake.

The odor that chased me in my sleep was at my face now. I pushed myself away from the stinking earth. My shirt and spicy *lei* reeked with vomit. I ripped off the shirt and the soiled *lei* and dropped them where I'd been sleeping.

I would get a clean shirt from my bundle.

My bundle! Where was my bundle?

Then I remembered that I'd thrown it at a wild pig. Thrown it and run. I began to hurry toward that place—that horrible grave I'd fled from before.

Could I find it?

Even if I found it, I could not go near it, could not visit that dreadful scene again.

But I had to. I couldn't live without that bundle.

I'd forgotten everything Kamaka had taught me about life in the woods. When I ran away from that grave, I hadn't paid attention to the trees and stones that would mark my return. I'd seen only a blur of trees and ferns and boulders.

The boulder! Where my bundle had landed, there was a large rock with moss on it. If I could find that rock, I could find my bundle.

The light was fading quickly, forcing me to slow down. But the dark shapes of trees and fallen logs were still visible. Whenever I saw a large rock I was sure it was the one. So I covered my nose and pushed my shaky legs forward. Still, I did not put one foot in front of the other without knowing exactly what I was stepping on.

Except for the odor, I might have tripped over the body. It was barely visible in the gathering darkness. When I smelled it, I turned to run.

But then I stopped. I reminded myself that running had only caused me problems. I would have to find a way to do this.

I would not look at the body. I would only look for the bundle. It was near a boulder that was green with moss. There it was; I was sure it was the same rock.

But I did not see my gray woolen blanket. I picked my way through the shallow ditch to the other side. I climbed over the large rock and searched the forest floor.

Where was my bundle?

I was in the right place. The rock was there. And the body. But the bundle had disappeared.

Terror burned like lava in my belly. It seized my arms and sparked to my fingertips. I was frantic. I couldn't leave without finding my bundle. And yet I could not stay in this awful place.

Perhaps in the morning, I told myself.

Slowly I backed away, tripping over a fallen log. I picked myself up, turned, and carefully chose each step. When I felt I had put enough distance between that grave and me, I found a bed of moss and curled up on it.

"At first light," I said aloud, "I will go back to where I threw up. To the place where I slept. I will find the shirt I took off, even if it's covered with vomit. I can wash it in a stream and use ginger sap for soap. After *that* I will find my bundle." I told myself these things over and over. It calmed me to hear them.

I closed my eyes and hugged myself to keep warm. But I did not sleep well, and when it was light, I awoke stiff and shivering. I didn't find the bundle or my shirt, although I found both of the places where I'd lost them. I saw that horrible body again. And some distance from there, in the place where I'd thrown up, I found the flower *lei*. I knew it was mine because it was soiled with vomit. But the shirt was gone.

Someone had taken a shirt that was soiled with my vomit?

I pounded my fist on the trunk of a tree. "My shirt," I moaned. "I need my shirt."

I wondered if the thief was hiding nearby. Was he crouching in the underbrush with my stinking shirt tucked under his arm?

If anyone needed it that badly, I should be willing to give it to him.

But I was desperate, too.

And so the thought of it angered me. "Thief!" I shouted. "I need my shirt. Bring it back to me!"

But no one came.

Had anyone even heard me? I really didn't know if anyone had followed me to this place, watching for a chance to steal my possessions. But if no one had, where had my shirt gone?

I turned and screamed to whoever might be listening, "You're evil, every last one of you. If you don't have something, you take it from someone who does. And now I have nothing!"

I leaned into the tree and rested my head against it. "Not even a shirt to cover my back," I moaned. "Not even a shirt. Nothing." I banged my forehead against the tree.

Then I turned again and looked at the moist green forest. And I looked beyond it, in the direction of the open peninsula and Kalawao village. Somewhere out there, I felt, there were more outlaws, all of them working against me.

What was it the man had said when he tried to take my bundle?

In this place there is no law.

What was he telling me? That the reason they came to the landing place was so they could prey on us? That everyone in this place was a criminal? Was that why the Board of Health put us here with high cliffs to serve as prison walls?

I knew that some of the missionaries believed that leprosy was God's punishment for breaking the commandments, as if having the disease meant we were criminals already. Kamaka's *tūtū* said that from the beginning they'd condemned many of our Hawaiian ways. Our clothing did not cover us well enough. The hula dance was sinful, and our gods and legends were too. The missionaries told us how to dress and what games we weren't allowed to play. We tried to obey them. But it was hard not to break their many rules.

Still, I did not know what crime I had committed. And now I would have to find some way to live in this place. Maybe I would become an outlaw too. How else could I survive?

I thought of the eyes that must be watching me now through the giant ferns and vine-covered trees. I wanted to hide on the forest floor, to crawl into the dark holes between rocks and tangled roots.

But this was no time to hide from prying eyes and listening ears. And so I announced my intention to those who'd followed me here, to the criminals who'd worked together to take my only possessions.

"You have taken everything from me!" I shouted. "I don't even have a shirt to wear. But I will find the things I need. I will get a shirt. And it might be yours!"

10

Ka Pōloli

[HUNGRY]

From that first day on Moloka'i, hunger chased me over the peninsula. It sent me to the ocean in search of fish and pushed me into the forest to scrounge for roots and berries.

I was excited to find *kalo* patches in one of the valleys behind Kalawao. But then I learned they belonged to people who were not part of the settlement. The people were willing to sell their *kalo* roots to leprosy patients. But their dogs would not allow us to steal from them.

Back on my island, we shared whatever we had with our neighbors. If a man needed a shirt, his friend would run home to get one. If a woman and her children were hungry, they simply went next door to eat *poi*. And if anyone, a friend or a stranger, needed a place to sleep, we were quick to offer our houses. "Let my little clump of grass be yours," we would say.

But here, on Moloka'i, our needs were too great. From the beginning, I had to learn new ways to survive. So I taught myself the location of each hut and learned which of the residents lived in caves. When they hobbled to the stream for water or searched the peninsula for fuel, I invaded their homes for what little food or clothing I could find.

I knew how wrong this was. But stealing was the only way I could survive.

The shirt I was able to take was too small. I tore new holes in it so the owner wouldn't recognize it and take it back. After my first day here I began to build a shelter but gave up when someone else invaded it and took a blanket I had stolen. I decided then to collect no more than I could carry.

I moved about the settlement like one of Hawai'i's legendary little people. According to our stories, the Menehune live in the mountains and come to the lowlands only at night. These short, hairy people work together to do good deeds for us, like building a wall or making a fishpond. They complete their task in one night and then disappear. Only a few of our people have ever seen them.

I wondered if the Menehune had built the many low walls that crisscrossed this peninsula. Maybe the stone walls had been enclosures for growing food. Or boundaries between neighbors in a long-ago time.

I tried to imagine the people who had lived here. Had they worked and played and fished and feasted together?

I saw that even now many of the people in this place stayed together for protection and helped each other out. Keona was one of them. She was the old woman who had rescued the little girl from Albert on the day I arrived. She and a group of friends looked after each other in true Hawaiian style.

I watched Keona and the little girl when I traveled near their thatched hut. But I was careful not to let them or anyone else see the things I was doing or where I was sleeping.

I often slept on the leeward side of a rock wall or beneath a shelter made with *kī* branches from the forest. And if it rained all night, I hardly slept at all.

Sometimes when the rains came I crawled under one of the houses in Kalawao. Of course, I had to be careful in the village. I did not want Boki and his helpers to see me there. But still I watched what went on in that place.

There was a *luna* who worked for the Board of Health and

tried to keep order. His house was enclosed in a dirty white fence along with a hospital and other buildings. There was even a jail, and on rainy nights I longed to sleep in that tiny building.

At other times I was afraid the *luna* would put me there for stealing.

Ah Loy and other young boys lived in one of the houses inside that fence. Another house overflowed with girls who desperately needed protection from Bad Albert, the octopus who'd tried to take the little girl at the landing place. Albert had his tentacles wrapped around every woman or girl who didn't have someone to look after her. And he didn't mind sharing them with other men in exchange for some *kī* root beer or a dip in their *poi* calabash.

There was even a schoolhouse in that picket enclosure. The teacher was one of the leprosy patients. But I did not see how anyone could learn reading or geography in this place, or why they would even want to. Food was the only thing that mattered here. And clothing and protection, and medicine.

The settlement had a hospital but no doctor to care for the sick. The *luna*'s wife did what she could, but mostly the patients lay on filthy mats waiting to die. I knew from the newspaper stories my mother had read that foreign doctors occasionally visited the settlement. But most were afraid to touch anyone who had leprosy, and none of them stayed.

We cared for ourselves as best we could, trying Hawai'i's plant remedies for our sores. And some of the Christians who lived here would go into the hospital and pray for very sick patients.

There were no real churches in Kalawao, but there was an American missionary, the Reverend Forbes, who came from over the *pali* once in a while. He'd preach to believers of the Protestant faith.

Mormons lived here too, and they had a priest who stayed

in the settlement. But his real reason for coming was as *kōkua*—to help his wife, who had leprosy.

And as far as I could tell, there was no one to preach to the Catholics. One day I heard several Catholics sitting on their porch discussing this problem. "We should sign a petition," one of them said. "We should ask the bishop to send a father to us."

I heard this because I was hiding beneath the porch, waiting for my chance to steal eggs from the chickens in their enclosed yard.

We mostly had to find or grow our own food. But the *luna* kept some cows, and one day some of the men helped him butcher a few of them. They distributed the meat to the patients, but it was gone before I decided to get in line.

The people took the meat to their huts, and the odors of it cooking drifted out their windows. I didn't know if I wanted to run away or move closer. Either way, the smell of food made my belly hurt.

I noticed that Keona and the little girl were eating with some friends behind one of the clapboard houses. The sight of them eating together made a tightness in my chest that ached almost as badly as the pain in my belly.

I had to get away from there, so I walked toward the sea. I sat on a black boulder and breathed in the smell of the ocean. The roar of the waves dashing against the rocks and the feel of the salty mist in my face made the food and the people in Kalawao feel very far away.

Tears stung my eyes as I thought of my family eating roasted pig and telling stories while we ate. I remembered how Kimi would snuggle under my arm and giggle in my ear. And how my mother would massage my shoulders while she talked.

I hadn't been touched since the day I came here, when the one-eyed Boki gripped my shoulder and offered to adopt me.

Many times I wondered if I should have gone to live with him. It would have been so much easier if I'd had others to help me survive on Moloka'i.

And in some ways I guess I did have others.

At least there was Ah Loy, who'd arrived on the boat with me. We never spoke to each other, but I watched him coming and going. And I learned in those first weeks that he was like a lizard hiding between the rocks, seeing everything that happened at Kalawao and reporting it to whoever would listen.

Early one morning, not long after coming to Moloka'i, I awoke to the sound of Ah Loy's voice. "Sail ho! It's Boat Day."

I'd passed the night in a corner where two stone walls came together. I waited until Ah Loy was safely past me. Then I stood and looked out toward the ocean.

The fog was so dense that I couldn't see a boat in the water. But still, I began walking toward the landing place. Waves of mist hovered white in the air about me, gently stroking my face.

Ahead of me I saw a few thatched huts, their sagging lines softened by the fog. They looked almost beautiful at this time of day before sunlight revealed how moldy and ragged they were.

They looked almost like homes in Honolulu.

Maybe I'm dreaming this, I thought. *Perhaps I'm not on Moloka'i. Maybe there's not a steamer in the bay. After all, I cannot see it.*

But then I did see it—the hateful little steamer that brought me here.

Like other Hawaiians, I'd always loved the steamers because they traveled between the islands. A steamer was supposed to take Kamaka and me to visit the big volcano. Instead, it brought me alone to this place.

I needed that steamer. It was the only way I could get the supplies my mother had promised to send.

When I thought about my mother's parcel I walked faster. What if some thief got to it before I did?

By the time I reached the landing place a small crowd had begun to gather. The healthiest patients and those who had a *kōkua* to carry them got there first. The helpers and even some of the stronger patients carried neighbors whose feet were crippled.

Keona was there with the little girl. The two of them sat on the rocks and waited to see what the boat would bring. I saw Boki and Albert scurrying up and down the ledge, lending their help to new arrivals. I stayed away from them, but as far as I could tell they were too busy scheming to even notice me.

The *luna* had brought his oxen with a cart attached. When the sailors unloaded cargo, they handed him wooden crates and large bundles of pounded *kalo* roots. A few of the patients helped pile them onto his oxcart.

If people tried to take something that didn't belong to them, the *luna* threatened to put them in his jail. But I noticed that Albert, Boki, and a few others managed to escape his notice.

Or did the *luna* just pretend not to see?

I watched for a package with my name. I was so intent on finding it that I was startled when a voice spoke into my ear. "So today you come for your government allowance? This is a good thing. Without your rations, you are skinny like a bamboo stick."

Rations? I jerked my head around to see who had spoken. It was Ah Loy, the annoying one.

He jabbed his finger at me. "Remember when we came here? Why did you run away? The *luna* sent someone after you, but you did not stop. So he gave your *poi* to someone else. Too bad for you."

"*Poi*? Food rations?"

"Did you think they shipped us here and forgot us?" asked Ah Loy. "They must send food. The *poi* is sour. The rice has bugs. But rotten food is better than *stolen* food. Don't you think so?"

I did not like the way Ah Loy emphasized *stolen*. But his news about government rations bothered me more. How foolish I had been! If I hadn't fled on that first day here, I wouldn't have lost my bundle to a pig and my shirt to a thief. I could have gotten food before looking for a place to sleep!

I knew I must not make such a mistake again. And so, after I found a crate from my mother, I joined the others outside the superintendent's shack. Ah Loy was right. The *kalo* roots the boss handed me were not fresh, and the rice was ridden with moths—but still it was food.

My mother had sent matches, soap, and tinned meat.

And a letter!

As hungry as I was for the food, I was even more starved for my mother's words. So I hurried away from the crowd that gathered around the *luna*'s hut. For some reason I went to the lone *hala* tree at the edge of the village. I settled myself on the ground and leaned against its trunk. Then I unfolded the paper.

My dear child,

We think of you every day. Yellow Cat reminds Kimi of you. She holds on to him all the time. I am sure that when she goes to school she will want to take him with her.

I worry over you. I don't sleep because I don't know if you are sleeping. I don't eat because I think you are hungry. There is no reason to smile now. Lani and Tūtū try to make me laugh, but I cannot.

Please write to me and tell me that you found

someone to live with. We will always be your true
family, but now someone else must adopt you.
Aloha Nui Loa from your mother

There were letters from Lani and Tūtū also. And a wilted
hibiscus blossom from Kimi. There was nothing from Kamaka.

I buried my face in the letter, hoping to breathe in the smell
of home. Trying to recall the look of my mother's face. But her
smile had disappeared, and without her smile I could not see her
at all.

I looked to the ocean and imagined swimming all the way to
Honolulu. That would put the sunshine back into my mother's
face. I thought how she would squawk at the sight of me. She'd
pull me from the waves and hold my face in her hands and laugh
and weep all over it. She would call for Kimi and for Kamaka
and his family too. Then we would all run to the hills, where the
sheriff would never find us.

But I knew that swimming to Honolulu was impossible.

Still, I sat on the side of that worn-out volcano and dreamed
I could do it.

I started thinking that if I couldn't swim there perhaps I
could climb the *pali*. After I reached the top, I could cross the
island and board a steamer bound for Honolulu.

And if they didn't allow me to buy passage? Well, then, at
least I could find a place to hide on the topside of Moloka'i.

I looked to the great green cliffs and wondered about life
at the top. I didn't know anyone who lived there, but I was
sure that beyond those cliffs were sunny villages with friendly
Hawaiian people.

I'd seen Mr. Meyer, the administrator who worked for the
Board of Health. He was a man with very little hair on the top
of his head but plenty of it growing on his face. He lived at the

top of the *pali* and came over the trail to check on the settlement from time to time.

I knew the trail was dangerous. But I'd climbed many cliffs and I began to dream about climbing this one.

If Mr. Meyer caught me he would probably have me thrown in the settlement jail. But what did I care? I was in prison already, shut away in this lonely place with no one to know whether I lived or died. I could not survive this way for long.

I kept reading and rereading that letter from my mother. I carried it wherever I went. Then one day, when I was drinking from a forest stream, it fell into the water. As I watched my mother's words slide into a blur, I felt that I was losing her all over again.

So I began searching the place in the distance where the ocean met the sky, watching for a steamer to come with another letter. But before the boat returned, I got sick. My nose ran, my head ached, and I coughed all night long. The sickness made me desperate to escape.

I left in the darkness of an early morning. Almost immediately the *pali* trail grew steep and then treacherous. In some spots it was completely washed out. Piles of sticks had collected in places where the trail should have been.

When daylight came I saw that I was leaving a trail of blood on the path. I examined my feet and found new sores in the numb areas behind my toes. Although I did not feel pain, I knew that I needed to protect my feet. I wrapped my handkerchief around the worst sores.

When I looked back to see how far I'd come, I was astonished to see how small the peninsula was. I had the feeling that if I kept climbing I could make it disappear completely.

I turned and pushed upward. I climbed steadily for a while. But then a fit of coughing came over me. It grabbed me by the throat and wouldn't let go. I clung to a small tree and coughed until my chest ached.

I peered through the leaves of the tree I hung on to. I saw nothing but blue beyond those leaves—the pale blue of the sky and the deep color of the sea. I could not see the peninsula anymore. I was relieved to leave it behind me.

But my legs were wobbly now, and I was weak and hungry. If I lost my balance I could easily fall and hit my head.

I was determined not to die while climbing this *pali*!

I turned to see the tops of those cliffs. And when I did, I saw what I did not want to admit. I was too sick to reach them.

This was what the Board of Health had counted on all along. They had picked the perfect place to imprison us.

I made one more start up the trail, but when the coughing set in again, I accepted their verdict. I turned and began the long journey back to the leprosy village.

And I just kept thinking as I forced myself down that hill, *I am doomed to live there for the rest of my life.*

11

Ka 'Ino

[STORMY]

I did not enjoy my life as a criminal in Kalawao. I could not get used to the guilt I felt. And I could never relax. I had to be careful not to let Ah Loy catch me snatching peas from someone's vines or sneaking eggs from under their nesting hens. He would be sure to report it.

But it wasn't Ah Loy who found me breaking into Boki's cookhouse. It was Boki himself.

Maybe I wanted him to catch me. But I was scared, too. I expected him to beat me when he found me shoving sweet potatoes under my shirt. Instead, he offered friendship.

"You are hungry," he said. "And I can get more sweet potatoes from my farm back in Kohala. Come live with me and eat your fill. I will adopt you."

Adopt me?

I hadn't trusted him when I arrived. But perhaps I'd been wrong. Why shouldn't he want to adopt me? Truly, it was the Hawaiian way. And my mother had told me to find someone to live with.

I was tired of moving from one place to another and weary of hiding my pitiful possessions. Although I didn't want to believe it, I needed someone. And so, in that moment of weakness, with Boki offering to become my *'ohana*, I agreed.

And then again, maybe it was the demanding look in his eye that held me there. And the way he placed himself between me and the door.

Boki's house was a small wooden building with two rooms, one for each of us. It had a shingled roof and glass windows that kept the rain out. Boki fed me roasted sweet potatoes and tinned salmon. He eased my aching throat with cups of cool water and hot tea. Then he pointed me to a mat with a warm blanket and told me to sleep until my cough went away. While he rubbed ointment into the sores on my feet I went to sleep.

But thoughts of Kamaka followed me. I dreamed that he tended my feet, scolding me all the while. "You have been careless, Pia," said Kamaka in my dream. "Too many of these mistakes and you will die. You should not have gone to Moloka'i without me."

Who was Kamaka to talk to me like that?

I had not run from him. *He* had run from *me*. And so I shouted in my sleep, "I can survive without you. I do not need you!"

But it was Boki who argued back. "You need me, Pia. You needed me from the moment you stepped onto Moloka'i. But I waited patiently and now you are mine."

Even through the fog of my sleep, I heard the mocking tone in Boki's voice.

When I stopped coughing and my head was no longer filled with thick fluids, he pointed me toward the cookhouse. "When I am hungry, you will cook," he said. He wagged a finger in my face. "After I eat, you eat. If I say so."

Then I knew for sure why Boki wanted to adopt me. It was not in the spirit of 'ohana, the spirit of family. It was in the spirit of selfishness that grew out of despair and anger. Out of frustration with the Board of Health, which was not taking proper care of us.

"Get this straight," said Boki. "I saved you from an early death. Now, you work for me. We're business partners. And never forget that Boki is the governor of this village."

And so I learned to awaken at first light, preparing his *poi* and coffee. I kept water in the barrel when the rain did not fill it. I scrubbed floors, cooked meals, and delivered messages to Bad Albert and Boki's other friends. And if Boki wanted me to steal something from another patient, well, I had to do that too.

I began talking to a few of the others who lived in the settlement, such as the little girl I'd met on that first day here. I learned that she never told anyone her real name, so everyone simply called her Maka Nui, Big Eyes.

I'd been watching her even when I avoided all the others. I noticed how Keona always kept her close by. The child was like a flower *lei* around the old woman's neck.

She was a generous woman, that Keona. Whenever I came near, she was quick to call out an *aloha*. And poor as she was, she often found something for me to eat or drink, even if it was only a bite of rice or a few swallows of coffee.

Keona's voice was sometimes hoarse from leprosy, but she did not let that stop her from sharing a poem or one of Hawai'i's ancient chants. I would sit on the earth outside her hut and listen to the rise and fall of her voice. And for those few moments I could believe that I was not sitting on the damp earth of Moloka'i. I could feel that I was on a clean, dry mat at home with my *'ohana*.

Keona and Maka Nui were the closest thing to family that I'd found in this place. After a while, I began to think that Keona would have adopted me as well. But it was too late for that. Boki would not let me go.

Keona had friends in the settlement. Some of them formed a Protestant congregation, and she was a part of it from the beginning. They didn't have a church building because there was no money or lumber to build one. But that didn't stop them from singing and praying together. They simply met on the *lānai* of one of the houses near the settlement's hospital. When the porch was full, they spilled out into the yard around it.

Sometimes I sneaked close enough to hear their singing. But listening confused me. One day it would make my life feel less lonely and the next time it would make me weep.

Boki didn't care for religion and wouldn't let me attend the services if I wanted to. But one day Keona asked me to go along. "The church is called Siloama," she said.

"That means Church of the Healing Spring," explained Maka Nui. "It's named after the pool of Siloama in the Bible— where a blind man was healed."

I could see that Maka Nui had been listening to the preaching of those Christians. "Tell me," I said to her and Keona, "has anyone been healed by going to your church?"

Keona didn't answer my question. Instead she quoted a bit of Hawaiian wisdom. "Be careful, Pia. Anger gives no life."

I thought I had plenty to be angry about. "You would be angry too," I said. "If you only knew."

"If I knew what?" asked Keona. "How it feels to be torn from the arms of my children and sent to the living grave? I know about that."

I just shook my head. Being taken from your loved ones was not the same as being rejected by them. But I did not tell her about Kamaka.

From my mother's letters I learned that Kamaka had gone to live at Kohala on Hawai'i's largest island and married a woman from there.

I wished my mother had not told me this. Usually I wanted her letters to contain more news. I didn't want to admit it, but I was always watching for Kamaka's name. Looking for word that he had come back to visit her. And for some sign that he cared that I was gone ...

But he had a new life now, a happiness that had nothing to do with me or even my family.

I was sure he had forgotten all of us.

I tried to forget him, too. But I couldn't. Everything I did to survive here reminded me of the things Kamaka had taught me. Even my dependence on Boki reminded me. I was like a young *kalo* plant that attached itself to an older corm. By now, I should have grown into the stem of a separate plant.

Why couldn't I learn to take care of myself? Why couldn't I be strong and fearless like Kamaka or truly mean like Boki? Then I wouldn't need anyone to help me survive.

12

Ka Mōhai

[SACRIFICE]

Sometimes I thought I missed Māui almost as much as I missed Kamaka. Life on Molokaʻi would be so much easier if I had a horse to get around on. If Boki was in a hurry for me to deliver a message, he often told me to take his horse. But Boki didn't like sharing anything that was his, and if somebody else had a good thing, he wanted that for himself too.

One day, after I'd been with him for a few months, he asked, "Why don't you have a horse? Every Hawaiian has a horse."

"I have a horse," I said. "But when the Board of Health brought me here they didn't offer to send him along."

"What?" yelled Boki. "You have a horse and you came without him?" He yanked a piece of paper from a drawer and thrust it in my face. "Write to your family. Tell them you can't survive on Molokaʻi without a horse."

"B-b-but my mother has no money to pay for his passage."

Boki didn't care about my mother. "She will find the money," he said. "Tell her to send the horse if she does not want bad luck to come to her child."

I didn't want to frighten my mother. But I had to write the letter. So before I asked for Māui I told her Boki lived in a *haole*-style house with glass windows and a shingled roof. I told her he had plenty of food. I did not tell her that he was blind in one eye. I didn't want her to worry that bad luck would come to me. And I especially did not want her to know that I lived with an evil man.

When the steamer came again, I sent the letter.

Until now, my mother had managed to provide some of the things I needed—clothes, paper for writing letters, and some ointments for my skin. But it was too much to expect her to ship my horse.

Still, the next time Ah Loy announced the arrival of a boat, I stood on Kalawao's shore, straining to see if Māui had arrived. First I had to wait for the whaleboats filled with new patients. It was raining and the sea was unfriendly, so the sailors worked extra hard to get them safely landed.

I was afraid the steamer would leave without unloading its cargo. But then I heard cattle bawling as the sailors pushed them overboard. Through the drizzle I saw the gray shapes plunging into the water. I saw a confused cow shake its angry head and turn out to sea.

In moments it faded into the fog. The crowd around me gasped. "*Auē*! The cow will die."

"We need the meat," moaned a man behind me.

We did need the meat. At any other time I would have regretted the loss of the cow. But on this day I was thinking only about a horse.

What about Māui? Was it possible he was on the steamer? Would they just push him overboard, too? And would he follow the cow out to sea?

"Oh, Māui, please come to me," I pleaded. I hurried over the rocks on the beach and waded into the surf. "Māui," I called, but I heard my voice blowing back to me. "Māui," I cried again. "Come—I am here."

I heard the sound of neighing. I saw a horse being pushed into the water. Was it mine? The horse turned away from Moloka'i, toward the open sea.

Auē! "No," I cried. "Māui, come to me!"

I knew that the horse could not hear my voice, and I could not see if it was Māui. But I screamed for him anyway. And then for some reason the horse turned. Turned and followed the cows that were swimming toward Moloka'i.

I watched as the horse fought the waves. "Māui!" I called again and again until he was so close that I heard his frightened snorting, saw him toss his head, and knew that it was Māui.

I feared he would not make it through the rough surf. I plunged deeper into the water, but a ferocious wave knocked me down. I scrambled to get up, and when I did I heard Māui's voice again.

I stumbled back to the rocky beach and waited, wet and shaking with cold, pleading for Māui to come to me.

The cows were stumbling onto shore now. The sound of their bawling was all around me.

But I was listening for Māui's voice. I shouted his name again and he answered. We called to each other like that until finally I knew that he was going to make it.

He surged forward on a violent wave and stumbled onto the shore. I grabbed his bridle and steadied him. And then I led him away from the water and leaned into his quivering body.

"*Aloha* to you, Māui. *Aloha* to you."

Māui whinnied softly and I stroked him. His horse smell made me think of Pele and Kamaka. But I pushed those thoughts away. "You're safe now," I said. "We are together again." When he stopped shaking, I led him up over the rocky incline onto the peninsula.

Boki met us at the top of the low cliff. "Such a pitiful steed," he sneered as he tossed a parcel to me. The bundle was wrapped in a mat tied with rope and dripping with seawater—the soaked possessions of an arriving patient. "Take these to my house," Boki ordered.

I did not look at the new patients to see who might claim the bundle. I simply tied it to the rope around Māui's neck. I climbed onto my horse and poked him gently. The people scrambled to get out of our way.

Behind me was the sea. Ahead was the green *pali* still shrouded in gray mists. The warm sun would not break over the cliffs of Moloka'i for hours. So the peninsula was as gray today as any day.

But to me, it was greener. The wind felt gentler. The *pali* seemed less like a prison wall. I thought I caught the sweet smell of flowers riding on the breeze. I breathed deeply and began to weep.

Māui had come.

As I rode, I could not stop crying. "Māui," I whispered as if speaking aloud would scare my horse away. "Māui, you are here."

I headed toward Kalaupapa, but I didn't enter that village. I turned instead and rode out to the windy northernmost point by the sea.

I stopped at the rim of black rocks by the shore and felt again my imprisonment. Even Māui could not take me away from this place.

Still, I closed my eyes and imagined that Pele and Kamaka rode ahead of me. I imagined the warmth of Kimi's face pressed into my back and her arms wrapped around my waist. I rode back and forth across the peninsula. I shut out the sight of scrubby grass and large black rocks. I tried to feel that I rode on the pale sands of Waikīkī.

But finally I had to return to Kalawao.

I rode past the settlement's graying buildings. A few of Keona's friends sat on a porch and visited with one another. They waved and called out to me as I rode by.

I saw the house for boys and the one for girls that were

enclosed in the same fence as the hospital. And the *luna*'s storehouse with the fenced-in area for livestock. Kalawao's residents milled about, swapping gossip while collecting supplies and letters from home. When it was my turn I asked the boss for my share of rations sent by the Board of Health.

"And Boki's too," I reminded him.

"Boki can come for his own rations," the *luna* grumbled. But of course he didn't want any trouble, so he gave Boki's supplies to me. When I turned away, he called me back. "You don't want your mail?"

I hadn't even thought about a letter. Māui would have been enough goodness for one shipment. I took my mother's letter and stuffed it in my pocket to read later.

I did not look at the residents who gathered outside the storehouse. But I could feel them watching me as I climbed onto my horse. I suddenly felt as tall and powerful as Hawai'i's king.

Before I could ride away a young woman was there by my horse's side. She grabbed at the bundle tied to the front of my saddle—the bundle Boki had stolen.

"It's mine," she said. She was smiling and crying at the same time. "It was so good of you to rescue it." Her hands trembled as she tried to loosen the knot I'd made. "Where did you find it? I was sure it had gone out to sea."

I knew she expected me to return the bundle, but I couldn't give it back!

Boki would abuse me. When I looked at the woman's hopeful face I wished I had taken it to him before coming to the *luna*'s storehouse. Now what should I do?

She tugged at the rope that tied her possessions to my horse. "Can you help me with the knot?" she asked. "This bundle has my clothes, my blankets, and my dishes. Some food, too. I *must* have those things." Her voice began to crack.

Should I return the bundle? Without it this woman might be forced to accept help from Bad Albert.

I could see him leaning over the fence that surrounded the *luna*'s hut. I saw the hungry way he was looking at her. As if *she* were the rations he had come to get.

For some reason I thought of Keona. Maybe she would help the young woman. I looked around but didn't see her.

"Ple-e-ea ease ..." The woman's voice was louder now, and yet it was breaking into little pieces.

I looked away. I slapped Māui's reins lightly and headed for Boki's house. Behind me, I heard an anguished cry. "*Auē!* Pleeeease give it to me." Her voice had turned to wailing now.

My first day on Moloka'i came back to me then. I remembered how losing my bundle had turned me into a thief. How it had made me a criminal who deserved to be locked up in this place. I hated myself for what I'd become.

Maybe it was this self-hatred that made me give the parcel back. Perhaps it was the joy of having Māui that changed me. But suddenly I didn't care what Boki did to me. I leaned forward and untied the rope that held the bundle. It bounced awkwardly to the ground. I did not look back, but still I could almost see the smile I put on that woman's face.

"I hope Boki has forgotten about that bundle," I muttered.

But he had not. He was waiting on the *lānai* when I arrived. "Where have you been? Did you think that sorry horse came here for pleasure riding? And where is that bag of rags I gave you?"

I slid to the ground and looped Māui's reins over a large rock beside Boki's house. "I must have lost it," I said.

"Lost it? Must I show you the only road that runs through Kalawao?" He grabbed me by the ear and dragged me into the road. He pointed to the ocean, which was so close that the sound of it was a constant roar. "Between the ocean and this house you lost it?" He shoved me to the ground.

"Shall I remind you who you work for?" He put his foot on my head and pushed it into the earth. "Look at me here!"

I could see only the sole of Boki's shoe covering my face. The stones on the road dug into my cheek.

"See me!" shouted Boki. "I am a hawk! I perch on the top of that *pali* and rule the rats that crawl in this dirt. Don't cross me again, Pia." He removed his foot, kicked me in the face, and stomped away.

I clutched my throbbing head. I heard the crunching of footsteps on the pebbles as neighbors left the *luna*'s house with their rations. No one stopped to help me. No one dared challenge Boki's actions. He was a hawk, and they did not want his talons in their flesh.

Only Ah Loy squatted in the dirt beside me. "That man," he said. "His real name is not Boki. He calls himself that because of that other Boki—the governor of O'ahu. He picked the name so other people will think he's in charge." Then Ah Loy lowered his voice and glanced back toward the *luna*'s storehouse. "I think Boki is the real boss here."

I wasn't so sure about Ah Loy's ideas. Governor Boki was a joke among the Hawaiian people because he'd been lost at sea and was never heard from again. "That will happen when Boki comes back," we would say when we thought something was impossible.

But maybe this Boki here in Kalawao approved of the governor. After all, both of them were greedy tyrants. Tūtū had told me how Governor Boki forced our people to work in the mountains for months—without proper food or shelter—collecting sandalwood so he could sell it to foreigners.

This was just the kind of man I would expect Boki to look up to.

I closed my eyes and turned my head, pretending not to hear Ah Loy. The boy only wanted to add insult to my humiliation.

I struggled to my feet but almost fell again. So I grabbed at Ah Loy to steady myself.

He put an arm around my waist. "I think the hawk almost killed the rat," he said.

I did not need to hear Ah Loy's opinions just then. But I could not stand up without him. Blackness swirled like thunderclouds in my head. I let him lead me to the water barrel behind Boki's house. Blood poured from my nose.

Ah Loy dipped water from the barrel and splashed it over my face. I slipped to the ground and leaned against one of the stone pillars on which the house was built. Pressing my nostril closed, I moaned as it filled with blood.

"Go away," I said.

Ah Loy did not move.

"Go," I said. "Find someone who hasn't seen my troubles. They will be glad for you to tell them."

"True," said Ah Loy. "I can take your horse, then?"

So that was why he stood there fastened to the ground like a tree! "No!" I growled. I reached for some loose pebbles and aimed them at Ah Loy. He backed away then, and I heard his footsteps grinding on the stones as he went around the side of Boki's house.

I sat there for a long time.

I wanted to run away, but leaving Boki would be impossible. There was no place to go. He would hunt me down and beat me. Or pay someone else to do it. I sat there and waited for my nose to stop bleeding. When it did and the throbbing in my head lessened, I reached into my pocket for the letter my mother had sent.

The blood on my hands smeared the page. But her words were still clear.

Aloha, my dear child,

Every day I weep for you. I dream that you lie in the rain with no roof. Then you write that you live with a man named Boki. I am happy that you're not sleeping on the earth and that you have plenty of sweet potatoes. They are not as good as poi *but at least they will fill your belly.*

If this man wants you to have a horse, you will have it. Tūtū sent a message to Kamaka. He paid Māui's passage but he sent someone else to take him to the steamer. He is ashamed to see me.

I crumpled my mother's letter in my fist. It angered me that Kamaka was the one who'd sent Māui to me. And I was even more furious that he would not speak to my mother.

Did he think that buying Māui's passage would put things right between us?

Kamaka was like the steamer that dumped me here and then brought supplies to me. He was like Boki, who rescued me and then made me his slave.

I hated all of them.

But I kept wondering—how could I survive without them?

13

Siloama

[THE HEALING SPRING]

Here on Molokaʻi, Boat Day always brings a feeling of anticipation. We never know what will come, but we're always hoping for news from home. And more supplies.

One day, two years after I arrived, the steamer brought something that surprised all of us. Or most of us, anyway.

Boki was in a hurry to get to the landing place that day, so we rode our horses fast—like missionaries with an important job to do.

Ah Loy did not have a horse, but as always he was there ahead of us. Sometimes I wondered if that boy ever slept!

Bad Albert was there too. I could see he was hoping to win the attention of some young woman who came off the steamer. He kept pulling a comb out of his pocket to rearrange his oily hair and tidy his mustache. And he stood so close to the water's edge, ready to grab whatever he could, that I thought he would be knocked down by the waves.

But Albert was not going to find a woman. We soon discovered that no new people were coming.

I was always relieved when the boat came without new patients. I never got used to the sight of weeping patients struggling onto our scrap of land. And I did not like stealing from them.

Boki grumbled when he realized there were no new patients to rob. He'd been bored and restless the week before and was looking for some distraction.

The steamer also did not bring crates of food or supplies sent by our families. So there was nothing for Boki to steal, but he didn't need to worry about excitement. There was plenty of it on that day.

I noticed that Keona and her friends had gotten there early. Even the ones who could not walk had been brought in wheelbarrows or carried on the backs of friends.

The Reverend Forbes came too. He was the American missionary who lived on the topside of Moloka'i and came for visits to Keona's congregation. On this morning he'd come down the trail with Mr. Meyer.

The *luna*'s oxen were there, attached to a cart. They snorted and bawled impatiently for their work to begin.

But what would they carry?

All of us were curious, but especially Ah Loy. The boy was squeezing himself into the little circle of believers as if he'd been attending their services all along. I watched his head moving back and forth as he followed their conversation.

After Ah Loy had gathered sufficient information, he left the little group and ran to some patients who had settled in the grass. He waved and pointed toward Keona and her friends. I thought I heard him say something about a church.

Soon he was standing before Boki and me. "They are bringing a church," he said. "The Siloama people are building themselves a church!"

Surely Ah Loy had misunderstood. I knew that Keona and her friends had tried to collect money for a church building. But money was scarce, and she had told me it would take a very long time. Here on the peninsula we never had enough food to eat or good houses to live in. And somehow this small group of people was building a church?

"But how?" I asked.

Ah Loy shrugged. "I'll be right back," he said. And he dashed over to the congregation. He elbowed his way into their midst again and tugged on the Reverend Forbes's arm until the man stopped talking and listened to his question.

When Ah Loy had the answer, he did not come right back to me. Instead he went to all the little clusters of people he'd talked to before.

I could see Maka Nui jumping from one foot to the next and twirling herself until she was dizzy. Her playfulness reminded me of my sister. I wondered what Kimi was doing just then, back at home in Honolulu.

Was she starting to forget me?

Maka Nui did not pay much attention to me, except to wave once when Boki was not watching. I wanted to go ask her how these Christians had gotten money to build a church. But I did not. And I knew she would not come to tell me. Not with Boki sitting beside me on his high horse.

After Ah Loy had shared his information with everyone else, he came back to stand in front of us. "They took up a collection," he said. "And the Reverend Forbes carried it with a message to topside." Ah Loy pointed to the top of the *pali*. "The Reverend sent the message to newspapers in Honolulu. Their friends collected more money and shipped the boards. The church people are very happy. Praises to the Lord!"

He started to go away then, but suddenly he stopped and said to me, "I gave you big news. Now you must give me something."

Give him something? Me? I supposed he thought I had things of value, since I lived with Boki. But he didn't know that Boki kept nearly everything he made me steal. I got only the things he wanted me to have.

Boki had wanted me to own a horse, and Māui was just

what Ah Loy wanted. "I need to ride your horse," he said. "To take this news to people in Kalawao. Some people are too sick to come and watch."

I was still thinking how to answer him when Boki reached down and swatted his ear. "Get away from here, you filthy beggar," he yelled.

Ah Loy grabbed at his ear and jumped back.

"Off with you!" Boki poked his horse with his knees, urging him toward Ah Loy. The boy jumped back again and fell in his hurry to get away. He scrambled to his feet and ran.

"And get that hair cut!" Boki yelled.

What did Boki think? That Ah Loy had a shiny pair of scissors in his pocket? If the boy had brought scissors with him to Moloka'i, Boki would have stolen them long before now.

The church came in many pieces. We watched the sailors toss bundles of boards over the steamer rail. The incoming waves carried the planks toward shore. As the boards neared the landing, the Siloama people—the healthier ones among them—waded into the water to rescue them. They worked together to carry them to dry land. Then they piled them onto the *luna*'s oxcart.

In this way the congregation brought a church to the peninsula.

Delivering boards was tricky enough, but getting a keg of nails onto the shore was even trickier. But Hawaiians enjoy working together. People who did not even attend the Church of the Healing Spring went into the water to help. Some were Mormon, some Catholic; others did not claim any religion at all.

Ah Loy was right there in the middle of the action. I guess he had decided not to tell the people back in Kalawao about the church that was coming on the steamer.

I wanted to help, too. I was climbing down from Māui when Boki stopped me. "You certainly will not help bring a church to

Moloka'i," he snapped. "What good has religion done anyone in this place?"

In some ways I agreed with Boki. I knew that the people of Siloama did not have more food or better houses than the people without religion. But sometimes I thought maybe they were wealthier than even Boki with all his stolen goods. At least they had each other.

"Well," I said, pointing to the smiling church members, "look at the people of the Church of the Healing Spring. At least their religion gives them some joy in this place."

Boki snorted. "Healing Spring! Such a fine name they give themselves. Tell me, where is their healing water? Are they going to tote their boards into the valley and hammer them together by the stream? Half of them can't even walk to get their own drinking water."

"No," I said. "They cannot. But the other half carries it to them. So I guess their religion brings them *some* good."

Boki laughed and slapped me on the shoulder, so hard that it hurt. "But look at me," he said. "I have no religion at all and I have *you* to carry my water."

I rubbed my hurting shoulder and did not say a word. I was thinking that I would much rather carry water for members of Siloama than be forced to get it for Boki.

But I could not leave Boki even if I wanted to join the Siloama church. I was his slave now, and he would make trouble for me. And besides, he was right about some things. The church people did not have good clothes, enough food, or warm houses. As long as I stayed with Boki I had all those things.

Keona's friends made many trips across the peninsula with their wood. Keona herself made only one. She stood in the grass where the people placed the boards and watched to be sure that no one took them.

When people came near the wood she called out to them. If they meant no harm she gave a friendly *aloha*. But if they seemed too interested in the planks or she believed they meant to steal, she'd stand in front of the pile and say, "This wood belongs to the Lord in heaven. And His all-seeing eye is upon you."

By this time Keona needed crutches to walk anywhere, so she could not chase any thief away from that pile of boards. Yet for some reason no one would steal from her.

I began to notice that Boki avoided her whenever he could. There was something about her that he seemed to respect. And I thought it was more than her threat about the eye of God.

But what?

Boki pretended not to be impressed by the church people, even though they worked just as hard to build the church as they did to get the boards, nails, and tools onto the shore. A man who was a carpenter was responsible for the building. But the church members helped. Some people who did not belong to the Siloama group also worked. After all, it was more interesting than waiting for the Board of Health to send a shipment of food and supplies.

Day after day the building continued, but Boki never went near. Instead he complained about the noise their hammers made. But I liked the noise. It reminded me of life in Honolulu. With a building going up, the settlement seemed more normal. And the sight of that little church with its steeple pointing to the sky seemed to bring new hope to us.

People left the valleys and came out of their huts, which were scattered across the peninsula. They straggled over to Kalawao village to watch the congregation work. And maybe they came to listen to the music.

One of the men in the church had a ukulele. He was blind, but that did not stop him from helping. He played his instrument and sang along while others worked. But he didn't sing by himself. Soon Keona and Maka Nui joined him. And others sang while they carried boards and hammered them into place.

I watched all of this as I rode about the peninsula doing Boki's misdeeds. The sight of those happy Hawaiians made my warm shirts and dry house uncomfortable.

At night those church people were in my dreams.

Or maybe it wasn't them.

The little girl with the big eyes was not Maka Nui after all—she was Kimi. And the woman who sang was not Keona but Kamaka's *tūtū*. My mother and Lani were there weaving mats and laughing while Kamaka hammered the roof onto the church building.

But then the hammering woke me. There was no singing or laughing or pounding of nails. Instead the windows were rattling as wind and rain beat against them. Not so far away, the ocean roared against the rocks until I feared it would escape its boundaries and come into our village. The night was so deep that I couldn't see the corners of the room.

I worried about Keona and Maka Nui in their simple thatched hut. I was sure they could not stay dry in this storm.

I closed my eyes, hoping to recapture the brightness of my dream. But thoughts of cold, wet leprosy patients and the sounds of Boki's ragged snoring would not let me sleep.

The joy I felt in the dream was not mine anyway. It belonged to the good people of Siloama.

My life was not about the comforts of religion or about working together in the Hawaiian way. It was about having enough to eat. And staying warm and dry on blustery nights. And sticking with Boki so I would not lose any of those things.

14

Ka Mokuāhana

[TO BE DIVIDED]

Living with Boki was like living with a Kona wind. One day he'd allow me to sleep in the middle of the day. The next, he'd work me with no rest.

But he kept me supplied with clothing and made sure I looked presentable at all times. If my hair grew too long he'd pull out scissors and order me to sit on his porch for a haircut. "You're starting to look like an outcast," he'd growl.

One day, in the year after the Siloama people built their church, he talked about his mother while he cut my hair.

"The Board of Health is killing her," he declared. "She was strong as *koa* wood before they sent me here. And now she is tender like a blade of new marsh grass."

I thought about my mother and how she had not slept for worrying about me. Was it possible that Boki also had a mother who cared for him? I tried to imagine him as a child. But I just couldn't. And I couldn't imagine Boki thinking of anyone besides himself.

He spat over the edge of his porch and said, "I refused to present myself at their detention center because my mother needed me. So they forced their way into our house and dragged me out in the middle of the night. She had no time to say a proper *aloha* and I could not make provisions for her welfare."

I thought I saw a tear in Boki's eye.

"At least she has Father Damien to visit her."

"Father Damien?" I asked.

"A Catholic priest," said Boki. "He has converted my mother to his religion. And he dips often into our *poi* because she thinks he is part of her *'ohana*. But nearly every family in Kohala has adopted Damien by now. So he's away much of the time. Traveling over the district to care for his flock."

I didn't see how a foreign priest could be much like family. Especially a priest who never stayed home.

I knew that recently a Catholic missionary named Bertrant had come to Kalawao to build a chapel. But he was like the priest Boki was talking about. He would not stay around for long.

Still, Boki had made me curious about his family. "What about the rest of your *'ohana*?" I asked.

"The rest of my *'ohana*?" Boki waved his scissors in front of my face—too close to my nose! "Apparently my brother has returned to manage my farm. He provides my mother with plenty of *my* sweet potatoes. I want her to have them. But a mother cannot live on food alone. She needs her son. And my brother is not her good son."

I laughed. "*You* were the good son?"

Boki leaned down so that he looked full at me with his one good eye. "Tell me," he said, "if *your* mother could see *you* now, would she call you her sweet little boy?"

I looked away then—out to the sea and beyond, toward my beloved O'ahu. "I was once a good person," I said.

"Sure you were," said Boki. "But who would know it now?"

His question made me wonder. Did Boki adopt me because he thought I was as bad as he was?

I knew I was angry. But that didn't mean I was evil. At least, I didn't think it did.

"The Board of Health has turned us into scoundrels," said Boki. "They should call it the Board of Death. They send us here to die. But we don't die from leprosy. We die because we give up on living. We die from gangrene and consumption, and dampness and starvation. At home we would be warm and well fed. But the Board of Death prefers this solution."

His scissors made threatening sounds close to my ears.

Boki snipped and snarled. "If they hide us away, visitors from Europe and America will bring money to our islands. If they don't, the travelers will take their money elsewhere. Then how would the government pay for its fine hotel?"

The fine hotel was the latest news in all the papers our families sent from home. Our government had built it. I wished I could see the grand building, and maybe even catch a glimpse of our king visiting with foreign royalty on the wide porch. But Boki did not wish to see the hotel. He wanted to burn it to the ground.

"They can't find the money to build huts for their own people in Kalawao," he complained. "And yet they can build a three-story hotel to entertain any foreigner with money in his pocket."

Boki was working himself into a vile mood. Suddenly he poked me in the back. "Why are you loafing in the middle of the day?" he demanded. He swatted clumps of hair off my bare shoulders. "Go bathe. Fetch us some water, too. The barrel is nearly empty. But first, clean up this mess." He kicked at the hair lying about on the floor.

I hurried to do as he commanded. Then I got the buckets and headed toward the stream. It was that time of day when the sun had finally reached the village of Kalawao. And getting away from Boki made it feel even brighter.

On the rocky road through the settlement I passed Brother

Bertrant, who was on his way to work on the Catholic chapel. One of the Catholic believers had stopped him at her gate.

I heard her begging him to stay in Kalawao. But he insisted that it wasn't possible. "I'm a Brother," he said. "I cannot perform the duties of a priest. I'll be leaving as soon as the chapel is built."

The woman would not give up on the idea of having a priest here. "Please," I heard her say as I went past. "Please, tell the bishop to send us a Father."

I had to hurry to the stream, so I did not wait for Bertrant's response. But I knew the woman's plea was useless. No minister would choose to come here if he were not forced to do so.

I passed the unfinished chapel with piles of shingles lying in the yard. The roof would soon be completed. Then Bertrant could leave us.

Ahead of me, out in the bay, I saw Ōkala, the small pointed island that poked its head through the deep blue water. I had often imagined swimming out there with Kamaka and climbing to its top. *We could plait some palm leaves and hang on to them while we leaped out over the bay. The winds would carry us, like birds flying.* I closed my eyes and imagined it. *If only Kamaka were here …*

But I didn't let myself think about swimming with Kamaka. Slowly I was learning to forget him. Soon I wouldn't think of him at all.

Before I'd gone very far, I met Ah Loy with a group of boys returning from the stream. His black hair hung in wet, limp strands on his shoulders. The other children were wet also. I supposed Ah Loy had ordered them all to bathe in the stream.

After they passed me, I heard him say something about Touch Hands. I knew he was talking about me. Touch Hands means thief. He probably felt it was his duty to warn the children about the bad boy who lived with Boki.

But they already knew about me. And they feared me, too. I could feel it in the way their chatter turned to silence when I passed them on the trail.

As I walked away from them, I thought about the things I'd done to make enemies in this place. "It's better this way," I told myself. "I don't need friends."

From Kamaka I had learned not to trust friends. They were like the slippery narrow pass I scrambled through on each trip to get water. Sometimes when the sea was violent, I couldn't go to the stream at all for fear of waves throwing me against the rocks.

The pass was friendly today because the sun was shining and the sea was calm. I stepped carefully on the least slippery spots and breathed a sigh of relief when I was safely on solid ground.

After a while I came to a place where a forest stream ran into the ocean. I could have collected my water without going farther. Instead I followed the stream up into the wooded valley. I loved these woods for the thick leafy greenness and the happy sound of water running over rocks. I would gladly have gone to get water every day if only Boki would allow it.

On this day, I crushed the bulb of a wild ginger plant and used the fragrant sap to lather my hair. After my bath, I dipped Boki's pails into a clear pool. Then I tied my bucket handles to the long pole I'd brought with me and hoisted them onto my shoulders. I turned and began the walk home.

When I was almost back to the settlement, I saw Keona and Maka Nui coming toward me. Seeing the two of them always softened the hard place inside me. If it weren't for them, I really would believe that enemies were better than friends.

Maka Nui carried her dented water bucket. The job was easy now because the pail was empty. But after she got her water much of it would slosh out along the way. Keona would not be able to help her because of her crutches. Even on a good day like this, the pass would be difficult for both of them.

"Stop," I said. I set my buckets on the ground and rubbed at my aching shoulders. "It's too far to walk. Take some of my water." I took the bucket from Maka Nui's hand and half filled it with water.

Keona gasped. "Sing praises to the Lord," she breathed.

"Will Boki beat you?" Maka Nui asked.

I wondered the same thing but did not admit it. "Oh, no," I said. "I'll tell him a thirsty shark stopped me on the trail and drank some of my water. Even Boki is afraid of sharks!"

Maka Nui laughed and wagged her head. Then she began to chant. "Boki's afraid of sharks. Boki's afraid of sharks!"

I grabbed her hands and we danced in a circle, chanting it together. We twirled faster and faster until Maka Nui's long, dark hair stood out behind her. And finally we collapsed on the grass and gulped big breaths of air.

Keona laughed. "Pia, it's good that you still have a soft place inside of you. Too much anger will kill you faster than any sickness."

I didn't want Keona or anyone else to tell me I shouldn't feel angry. So I said, "I have to go now. Boki will become meaner than a thirsty shark if I'm late."

I picked up my buckets and walked toward Kalawao. I stopped only for a moment to stare at Brother Bertrant working on the new church.

He'd chosen to build the chapel close to the only tree in the village, the young *hala* I'd noticed on my first day in this place. It offered very little shade, but some of the villagers sat beneath it to watch the missionary and those who helped him. Others sat on black boulders or sprawled on the grass. They were pleased to have another church in Kalawao.

"Two churches in this place!" said a woman. "Imagine that!" It was the same woman who'd been begging for a priest when I passed her house on the way to get water. She must have followed Bertrant here to see his progress.

"Yes," I said. "The Protestants have a church, so I guess the Catholics had to have one too. But no minister for either one," I reminded her. "They come for short visits. They say their prayers and leave again. The rest of the time, this new church will be closed."

I suppose Bertrant heard me complaining because he called out to me from the roof where he was working. Then he scrambled over the side and climbed down his ladder.

I tried to hurry away before he could speak to me. But I only managed to spill water from Boki's buckets. I slowed down and soon I heard a voice in my ear.

"You must come to the chapel when it's finished. It will be a place for you and the others to receive the sacraments."

I stopped and looked at the missionary. "Sacraments?" I asked. "What your people need here is a place to sleep. Will your church be open when the next Kona wind comes through? And where will *you* be then? Warm and dry in Honolulu?" I didn't wait to hear what he had to say. I just hurried away with my buckets of water.

Bertrant was probably praying for my soul. He would never guess what I was like before coming to this place. But what did I care what some Catholic priest thought of me? I was a Protestant. Or I had been, anyway.

By now, I was no kind of Christian at all.

15

Ka Pū'iwa

[SURPRISE!]

The days were short in Kalawao because the sun did not appear over the *pali* until nearly noon. The nights were long and wretched. Blustery winds seemed to leak into every corner.

Somehow the misery added up to four years. Then in December of 1872, during my fourth year at Kalawao, Hawai'i's king died, the one who had established this settlement.

The new king dismissed the Board of Health and appointed another one. According to the stories we got from newspapers and our letters from home, the new board was determined to find everyone on our islands who had leprosy. More bounty hunters were sent out to track them down. And the rumors must have been true because the steamers came more often and brought larger groups of people.

There was much to gossip about in Kalawao as more huts were built along the road between our village and Kalaupapa.

Mr. Meyer visited the settlement more often. He went from house to house with the *luna*, ordering everyone who didn't have leprosy to leave the peninsula. "The Board of Health cannot afford to keep you here," he said.

Of course those who'd come to help sick family members couldn't just leave them. Some helpers did because they were forced to. Others hid.

We learned to expect new changes each week. But one day when the steamer arrived it brought something that jolted me, as if a volcano had erupted. And like the earthquakes that follow an eruption, it shook me for days afterward.

The day began like all other days—with Boki ordering me about from the next room.

"Pia!" he called. "Come here, Pi—" Boki interrupted himself with a gurgling cough, an insistent noise that interrupted my sleep. I shook my head, trying to bring myself awake.

I pushed back my blanket and stumbled into his room. Boki lay in his bed, coughing too hard to yell. But his sickness did not stop him from being demanding.

"Water."

I reached through his window and dipped a tin cup into the rain barrel that stood under the eaves. I carried the cup to Boki and waited for him to stop coughing. Then I turned to head back to my own room.

"Stay," he croaked.

I stopped in the doorway and wished that I'd poured the water over his head. I felt myself going back to sleep there on my feet. But I pulled myself awake and went to my own room for my blanket. Then I came back and lay on Boki's floor.

I wondered if Boki was dying. He'd been coughing for months, and I'd tried to heal him by making tea from *māmaki* leaves. But I couldn't tell if the tea was helping.

There'd been so many times in the last four years that I wished he were dead. Now his death seemed almost within my reach, and suddenly I was worried.

How could I survive without Boki?

"Water, Pia, water ..." I drifted off to the sound of Boki calling. But I didn't get up. I settled into sleep and watched as he lay at the edge of a boiling volcano. Gleaming red lava splashed onto his flesh. He screamed and pleaded for relief. I stood just out of his reach with two shiny buckets of water.

Boki reached with desperate hands. But when he did, they were not his hands; they were the strong hands of a healthy man. I looked into the man's face then and saw two bright eyes. It wasn't Boki after all. It was Kamaka.

He wasn't lying down as Boki had been. He stood on the rim of the crater with Pele's fire glowing along his body. Kamaka's hair was long and curly and edged with fire. His face was covered over with smiles. "Pia, let's go for a swim," he said.

Suddenly I felt my power. Kamaka wanted my friendship. But I did not want his.

I looked at him and smiled a slow, taunting smile. Then I poured the water down the side of the mountain and watched it turn into a cool stream. It rippled over the rocks like an old song. But it was not a happy sound.

"Swim by yourself, Kamaka," I said. "I will never swim with you again."

The volcano erupted then and shook me awake.

Boki's hand was hot and shaky on my shoulder. "Water," he demanded.

I jumped to my feet, surprised to realize that Kamaka was only in my dream. I filled a cup with water and held Boki's head while he drank it.

The moonlight had disappeared into the misty layers of a Kalawao morning. I heard a voice outside. "Sail ho! It's Boat Day. Kalaupapa landing place."

It was Ah Loy running the paths of Kalawao with the announcement. Sometimes I wondered how the people managed here before he came.

If the seas were calm the boat arrived close to Kalawao. But when they were not, it unloaded at Kalaupapa, on the healthy side of the peninsula. With Ah Loy calling out the location, I could be sure to go in the right direction.

Boat days were the only times we were allowed to go to Kalaupapa. And even then we had to stay away from the villagers.

When Boki lay back on his pillow, I said, "It's Boat Day. I guess I'll go to the landing and see what I can steal."

Boki had fallen back to sleep. I refilled the cup with water, set it on a small table, and dragged the table to Boki's bed so he could get his own water.

Then I washed my face, pulled on my trousers, and changed my shirt. I took a cloth sack off a nail on the wall and slipped quietly out the door.

I climbed onto Māui and rode to Keona's small thatched hut. "It's Boat Day, Maka Nui," I called. "Are you going?"

Maka Nui came to the door. Her long hair was tangled like seaweed.

"*Aloha* to you, Pia. Can I ride on your horse with you?"

"Of course," I said. "But you need to comb your hair first."

Keona came to the doorway. Her hair was loose and needed combing too. But none of this changed the beauty I saw in her. Somehow the light in her eyes always made me want to stay and visit.

"Pia, you watch her. Don't let Albert get close to her or I'll feed you to the wild pigs." Keona combed Maka Nui's hair while she talked. Then she tied it back with a bit of plant fiber. "There, now you look better." She gave Maka Nui a playful swat on the bottom.

Maka Nui did look neater, but her dress was wrinkled. It was the same one she'd slept in, and one of the buttons was missing.

I wished I could go to the marketplace and buy her a new dress. But there was no market in Kalawao. And I had no money. I hoped her family would send her some clothes on this shipment. But she didn't usually get much from home.

"Watch for a box with my name on it," said Keona. "My sister is sending me coffee and newspapers."

I helped Maka Nui climb up behind me. She wrapped her arms around my waist, and we headed across the plain.

"I can't see the boat," said Maka Nui.

"That's because it's foggy."

"But how do you know it's there?"

"Because Ah Loy said so and he knows everything about this place."

"Does he know who's coming on the boat today?"

"Nobody knows that."

"I bet it's more people with leprosy."

"Probably," I said. I hurried Māui along then because I was anxious to see if anything had come on the boat for me.

Maka Nui leaned her head against my back. She didn't speak for a while and I thought she might be falling asleep. But suddenly she spoke up. "Pia," she said, "your foot is bleeding!"

I looked at my foot and saw that she was right.

"There are thorns by Boki's house," I said. "I must have stepped on them."

"Doesn't it hurt?"

"I can't feel it."

"Can you feel me here at your back?" asked Maka Nui.

"Of course."

"I can feel it too." Maka Nui leaned into my back. "I like you, Pia."

I liked Maka Nui, too. I liked the way she felt like family to me. "Good," I said. "Because if you don't like me I'll throw you into the Kauhakō Crater."

I turned Māui back toward the hill that had once been a volcano. Maka Nui knew that in ancient times the crater inside had sometimes been used for a watery grave.

"No!" she squealed. "Don't take me there. I like you, I like you! Don't take me there." Her voice jiggled because we were riding fast.

I slowed Māui down. "All right, then," I said. "I won't throw you in the crater after all. I'll take you to the landing instead."

We rode across the peninsula, and I noticed how the lantana spilled over the low rock walls. And how its tiny blossoms of yellow, orange, and pink were so vivid against the scrubby plain.

I also thought how odd it was that these flowers had been here all along. All I had seen at first was the grayness of this place. But now it seemed that making a few friends had helped me notice patches of color splashed across our peninsula.

When we got to the landing, others were already there. They sat on black boulders or lay in the scraggly grass and waited for letters and supplies from home. And food sent by the Board of Health.

I saw the first whaleboat being loaded from the side of the steamer. For a moment I felt sorry for the people climbing into the little boat. But then I remembered to harden my heart so that I would not feel their pain.

I helped Maka Nui climb down onto a lava boulder and then I hopped off Māui, tied a rope to his halter, and looped it over the boulder. I sat down to inspect my wounds.

I found two thorns near the middle of my right foot. That was when I realized that the numbness behind my toes was spreading. I pulled out the thorns and wiped away the blood that oozed there.

I was glad that at least I didn't feel pain. But I told myself to wash the wounds as soon as I could. And to treat them with salt and the juice of *pōpolo* berries. But first I must pay attention to what goods might be coming from home.

I watched the whaleboat as it came closer. I saw a man and

woman huddled in the boat. It made me feel again how alone *I* was when I came here. It reminded me of how Ah Loy and the sailor had said it was good to stick together. And how, in some ways, Maka Nui, who'd been a stranger, became my little sister on that day.

But this man and this woman didn't look like strangers who just happened to be in the same whaleboat. They looked as if they'd chosen to come here together. Still, from the way she hung on to his arm I thought she was afraid of losing him before they arrived.

The woman raised her face to the high *pali*. She reached for the *lei* around her neck and pressed its purple blossoms to her face. Even from this distance I could see how she clung to it. And how it shook in her hands.

It was probably her last gift from her family.

The man who was with her did not look at the *pali* or pay attention to those of us waiting on the shore. Instead he stared into the waves at the side of the boat. I suppose he was thinking how each wave carried him closer to Moloka'i. And farther from home.

He was a tall man and his broad shape was familiar. I couldn't see his face. But his hair—it was curly. And I felt suddenly as if—as if …

As if someone I knew was coming to the leprosy settlement.

I could not believe what I was seeing! I grabbed Maka Nui's hand. "Surely it's not him," I said.

"Who?" asked Maka Nui.

I noticed how the man lifted his head. How he saw the people of the settlement watching him. How he blinked, then closed his eyes quickly, as if that would erase what he had seen. He pulled the woman's face into his chest then, as if he wanted to prevent her from seeing it, too.

So tender he was and so much like family!

"Tell me, Pia!" said Maka Nui. "Who do you see?"

"I think I see someone I know." My voice trembled and I hugged myself to control my shaking.

"Who?"

Maka Nui tugged at my arm, demanding to know what had disturbed me so.

"K-K—Kamaka," I said. "I see Kamaka. But why is *he* coming to Kalawao?"

16

Ka Hōʻole

[TO DENY]

"I told you the boat would bring more people," said Maka Nui. "Didn't I tell you?"

I stood and walked away from the landing. I wanted to run to the Kauhakō Crater and hide inside.

"Wait, Pia. We didn't get the coffee for my *tūtū*. Where are you going?"

I stopped. Maka Nui was right. I couldn't run. I was not a frightened child. I was a man now, and I had responsibilities. I smacked my fist into the palm of my other hand. I forced my head up and marched defiantly back to the landing.

I put stone in my heart and caution in my head. *Leprosy is making me numb*, I reminded myself. *I feel nothing. And Kamaka cannot hurt me.*

But why is he here? I wondered. *Does he have leprosy too? Big, strong Kamaka?*

I watched him slip over the side of the small boat. I saw him reach his strong arm to the woman who was with him. She clutched a parcel with one hand and hung on to Kamaka with the other.

Kamaka braced himself for an oncoming wave, and when it passed, he lifted the woman from the boat. He held her while the water washed over her shoulders. Then he carried her over the black lava rocks of the landing place. Her blue calico dress left a trail of water and seaweed across the sand. Kamaka put her on the ground. Her teeth clattered with the cold and he massaged her arms.

He picked a bit of seaweed from her hair.

When he did that, I could feel his tenderness toward *me*. Could feel how he carried me on his back when I was still small. How he picked bits of coral from my knee when I fell in the marketplace. And much later, on that morning in the mountains, how he pulled me away from the man with leprosy.

Kamaka had tried to protect me. But somehow, he had failed.

His woman looked around her, and I turned away quickly before she could see me. I didn't want her to be horrified by the lumps in my skin or the ear that had begun to swell.

But I couldn't help myself. I couldn't stop looking at them. I had to know what Kamaka was doing here.

He turned then and looked at the crowd at the landing place. What was he looking for? Who was he looking for? But he didn't look in my direction, and he didn't look at any of us for long.

I saw that he stared out to sea—toward Oʻahu. Was he hoping to see Diamond Head in the distance? Was he afraid he would never see it again?

I felt a sharpness in my throat and a sting in my eyes.

No! I reminded myself. *I will not cry. I cannot feel.* I kicked a boulder to convince myself I did not feel the pain.

"Are you mad, Pia?" asked Maka Nui. "Why are you mad?"

I took her hand and turned to watch as sailors on another whaleboat began to unload supplies. "No," I replied. "I am not mad. I do not feel anything."

But I *was* mad. I was mad that Kamaka would see how I lived here. Angry that he would find me this way, weak and dependent on Boki. I didn't want him to know that I was not surviving just fine without him.

"It's time for the crates," said Maka Nui. "Now they will bring Tūtū's coffee."

I tried to watch for a crate with Keona's name on it. But I kept glancing at Kamaka and that woman.

I didn't know how I could find Keona's box without Kamaka seeing me. My neighbors scrambled all over the landing place, snatching up crates labeled with their names and pestering the superintendent for their rations.

I found Keona's crate. And a parcel with my name, too. I picked them up and turned to leave, nearly forgetting to steal something for Boki. But then I saw something else—a crate with Kamaka's name.

Of course! I could steal that. It wasn't enough to show Kamaka how angry I was, but it was all I could do for now.

I looked around, but I could not see Kamaka through the crowd. I quickly opened his crate and dumped its contents into my sack. I kicked the box aside, hoisted Keona's crate onto my shoulder, and picked up the bag.

"Let's go," I said. "Hang on to my sack and don't let go. If we get separated, Keona will feed me to the pigs."

Maka Nui followed me through the crowd. I led her back to the place where we'd left Māui.

But—Kamaka! He had seen Māui and was there ahead of me. He stroked my horse's face. And leaned into his neck. I could tell from the way Māui tossed his head in that slight rounded motion that he was glad to see Kamaka.

Suddenly I wished I had left Māui back at Boki's house. Why, today, had I brought him to the landing place?

But then, I never expected Kamaka to come on that steamer. I just stood and watched and didn't know what to do. The woman saw me staring and tugged on Kamaka's arm.

Kamaka lifted his head then.

I wanted to run. But I fastened my feet to the ground and crossed my arms in front of my chest to show him I was not afraid.

When he saw me, he reached for the woman.

Up close like this I could see the red patches of leprosy on her neck. She was losing her eyebrows, but her eyes were deep and beautiful. I noticed that along with the purple *lei*, she wore Catholic prayer beads around her neck. When Kamaka reached for her, I wondered, *Who is he protecting—himself or the woman?*

"Pia, it's you," he said, his voice so soft I almost didn't hear him. "I'm so glad to see you."

I saw how he looked at me. And how quickly he turned his head away.

Does he have leprosy? I wondered.

But Kamaka didn't appear to have leprosy. His skin was brown and smooth, as always. Then again, he did not walk with his shoulders back and his head held high. The shine in his eye was missing. And his laughter—where had it gone?

Was this person really Kamaka?

Maybe that is why I could speak so boldly—as if I was only being rude to a foreigner. "Really, Kamaka? Are you truly glad to see me? Look at me, then. Do you like what you see?"

Kamaka flinched. He looked past me, to the ocean.

So I kept up my attack. "I always wanted to be just like you—so fearless. Now, are you afraid, Kamaka?" I moved in closer, pushing myself into his view. "Are you afraid you will become just like me?"

Kamaka looked at me then. He opened his mouth, but no words came. He backed away and gripped the woman's shoulder so tightly that she winced.

"Who is it?" the woman asked him.

In spite of the way he hung on to her, Kamaka seemed not to realize she was even there. "Pia," he whispered. "Pia, I *am* glad to see you."

And this time he did not look away.

It sounded as if he meant it. But was it true? Did he really care?

I laughed then, to cover my pain. It was more of a snicker, really—a bitter sound that reminded me of Boki.

Kamaka reached out to me. But I jumped back as if a touch from him would destroy me. I bumped into Maka Nui.

"Ouch! Pia, you stepped on my foot. Who is that man? Is he your friend?"

I grabbed Māui's reins and led him away from Kamaka. I lifted Maka Nui onto my horse and tied Keona's box on behind her.

Kamaka did not leave and he did not come closer. He didn't speak. He just watched. I climbed onto Māui.

"No," I said, looking down at him. "He is *not* my friend." I dangled my sack just out of his reach. "You ought to guard your possessions more carefully," I said. "And don't let go of that woman. We have an octopus here who will gladly wrap his tentacles around her."

The woman cried out and thrust both arms around Kamaka. I felt almost sorry for frightening her like that. But I knew I could not become soft now. So I took a deep breath and, just like one of the settlement's worst criminals, I announced, "In this place there is no law."

I did not look at Kamaka's face when I said it. I could not bear to see his eyes when he saw that I was a thief.

"Let's go, Maka Nui," I said. "Your *tūtū* is waiting for her coffee." I slapped Māui with the reins and we headed across the peninsula.

Behind me, I heard Maka Nui asking questions. "Pia, who is that man?" she asked. "Do you know him? And the woman—who is she?"

I heard the questions, but I wasn't really paying attention. I was just trying to get away from Kamaka. But Maka Nui kept asking.

"Pia, talk to me. Why are you mad? Do you know that man?"

I wished that she would be quiet. I could not think with all her questions. I could not figure out what I was going to do now that Kamaka had come to Kalawao. I had enough questions filling my head already. I did not need hers, too.

"Hush!" I shouted at her. "Would you stop asking so many questions?"

Maka Nui became very quiet then. And I felt her pull away.

Māui picked his way around a large black boulder. A frightened mongoose scooted across our path.

The distant sound of the ocean felt closer than usual.

Suddenly Maka Nui's quietness bothered me more than her questions had.

I felt bad then for hurting her feelings. She was tough—she had to be, to survive in this place. But she was still a child, and she deserved to be treated gently.

I climbed off Māui and lifted Maka Nui to the ground. I knelt and brushed strands of hair from her face.

"Look," I said. "I don't know about that man. Probably he is a kōkua—you know, someone who came along to help his woman."

I didn't think this was true, since the Board of Health no longer allowed patients to bring helpers with them. So I added, "Or maybe he has leprosy. I don't know why he came to Moloka'i."

"But why are you mad at him?"

"I am mad because of leprosy. When some people find out you have it, they don't like you anymore. Doesn't that make you mad?"

Maka Nui nodded. "But, Pia, mostly I am mad when you yell at me."

"Oh, Maka Nui," I said, "I'm sorry. I promise not to yell at you again."

I lifted her onto the horse—toward the front this time—and climbed on behind her. I gave her the reins and said, "Take us home, Maka Nui."

She giggled and slapped Māui with the reins. Then she leaned into my chest and we rode across the peninsula.

We found Keona sitting by her hut, soaking her feet in a tin basin of ash and salt water. She'd been doing that a lot lately. It was a remedy she'd read about in one of Hawai'i's newspapers. I gave her the box from her sister and helped Maka Nui to the ground. "Here's your girl, safe as when you last saw her. I didn't even notice if Albert was at the landing."

"Who did you see?" Keona asked. "Did something good come on the boat today?"

I shook my head and waved goodbye to Maka Nui. "No," I said as I turned Māui toward the leprosy village. "Your coffee was the only good thing."

17

Uku Pāna‘i I Ka ‘Ino

[REVENGE]

Boki was on the *lānai* when I got back. "Where have you been?" he snapped. "I could have died while you were gone."

"No," I said. "You're too mean to die. What would Kalawao do without you to make trouble? The superintendent would be out of a job."

Boki chuckled. "That's what I'm training you for," he said. "If you haven't learned a thing about crime by now, just let me know and I'll teach you today."

I turned my sack upside down and dumped its contents on the porch floor. It was filled with the predictable household utensils, a bunch of *kalo* root, tins of meat, and a looking glass. And there were smaller parcels wrapped in fabrics and bound with rope.

Boki kicked most of the items aside. "Cups and knives?" he sneered. "Are these trifles the best you could do?" But in spite of his grumbling, Boki was glad for every little thing he could get. He would trade cups and knives for services from his neighbors.

He picked up one of the smaller parcels and untied the fibers that held it shut.

"Books," he said. "Someone reads—or at least they did. I'll be the one who's reading now." He tossed the fabric aside and inspected the books, naming several titles as he discovered them. *"Pride and Prejudice. Catechism of the Catholic Church."*

He threw the religion book onto the floor. "You can burn that one," he said.

I did not see what other books there were. But I put the catechism aside. I would keep it in my room until I could trade it for something I needed more.

A small crowd was coming down the road with the *luna* leading the way on his horse. He always took new arrivals to his storehouse for supplies.

In moments, they were in front of Boki's house. The *luna* glanced briefly at Boki and gave him a curt nod. He fingered the gun he carried in front of him.

Boki chuckled softly. "The *luna* thinks I'm afraid of his gun."

I wasn't concerned with the boss. *I* was thinking about Kamaka. I could see him at the back of the group, the tallest person there. He looked as bewildered as all the others.

I studied the woman who was with him. She was just the kind of woman Kamaka would choose—not the perfect Hawaiian, large and commanding, but someone small and delicate who would depend on his strength. I realized that it was not only she who needed him. Kamaka needed her as well. He needed her to make himself feel strong.

The woman stumbled over a stone in the road, but Kamaka caught her before she fell. The crowd moved out ahead, leaving the two of them alone in front of Boki's house.

Boki began a low cursing and I realized he was watching Kamaka and his wife.

"Do you know them?" I asked.

"That," snarled Boki, "is Malia—the woman who sent me to Moloka'i! *She* told the sheriff I had leprosy." He leaned forward and studied her with spiteful eyes. "But the devil is my best friend for sure. If I hadn't left my mark on her she wouldn't be here." He rubbed his hands together and began to laugh.

And when he laughed I felt fear for the woman. It was bad enough to arrive on Moloka'i without knowing anyone here. It was much worse to come here and have an enemy already. Especially if that enemy was Boki.

His menacing laugh changed to a slight cough and then into a strangled fit of coughing.

Kamaka hadn't seen us there on the *lānai* until Boki made so much noise. At first I thought he would come and demand his possessions while the *luna* was nearby with his gun. But then the woman recognized Boki. She turned her face away and pulled the blanket over her head. She tugged on Kamaka's arm, leading him away.

"Water!" demanded Boki.

I scooped up the *Catechism of the Catholic Church* and took it into my room. I tucked it under my mattress. Then I filled a cup with water and gave it to Boki.

The new arrivals had moved on. I saw only Kamaka's back now, his bowed head and the sag of his shoulders.

Boki cleared his throat and spat onto the floor of the *lānai*. "Follow those two," he ordered. "If they try to build a house, destroy it. If they plant a garden, tear it up by the roots. We'll show them just how miserable life on Moloka'i can be."

I smiled. For once Boki and I shared a vision. I imagined our revenge to be as sweet and juicy as the bright yellow flesh of a ripe mango.

"And one more thing," said Boki. He spoke slowly. "Every Friday afternoon, take a roasted sweet potato to that woman. Tell her it is a reminder from an old friend."

For some reason, when Boki said that, the thought of ripe mango put a rancid taste in my mouth.

18

Ka ʻUala

[SWEET POTATO]

At first, after Kamaka arrived, I avoided him. But that didn't stop me from watching. I saw him settle with his wife in one of the rock wall enclosures out on the plain, near the Kauhakō Crater.

First he made a temporary lean-to, and then he began to build a sturdy thatched hut. He must have believed what I said about Bad Albert, because I noticed that he never left Malia alone.

I supposed Maka Nui had told Keona all about Kamaka. Right away his wife had begun to spend time at Keona's hut. And Keona must have told her church friends, because some of them helped Kamaka build his house.

I stopped by Keona's hut less often now because I did not want to bump into Kamaka or his wife. But on the first Friday after they arrived, I couldn't avoid them.

First I had to cook some sweet potatoes. Boki picked the biggest one in the pile. "Give it to Malia," he said. "And I want a report when you're done."

So I went to the slope of the Kauhakō Crater and sat to watch, waiting for my chance to deliver Boki's revenge. I pulled my mother's letter from the pocket of my trousers. It had arrived on the same day Kamaka did. On that day, I'd waited until after the new arrivals left the superintendent's house. Then I went for my rations and my mail.

I read it again.

Dear Pia,
 Now it is Lani and Tūtū who weep without ending. They say they will never see Kamaka again. I tell them he will return someday. I tell them maybe his wife does not have leprosy after all. I say all the things they said to me when you went away. But they will not believe any of it.
 I try to make them smile, but they say there is nothing to smile about. They are right. I am not smiling either. I don't even try to cheer them up anymore. My only pleasure is knowing that you and Kamaka are together again.
     Aloha Nui Loa from your mother

Kamaka and me together again?

I would let my mother believe it. After all, there were many things on Moloka'i that a mother should not know. My hatred for Kamaka was only one of them.

After reading the letter again, I sat on the slope of the crater and watched as Kamaka climbed onto Pele and helped his wife climb up behind him.

It hurt to see Pele. I had convinced myself that having Kamaka on Moloka'i did not make me feel anything. But then Pele had arrived in a shipment of beef cows. It was another reason to avoid Kamaka—so our horses would not meet.

But Pele had announced her arrival with a loud whinny, and Māui had heard it. He had been restless ever since. The sound of them calling to each other was almost more painful than the sight of Kamaka himself.

Now Kamaka turned Pele toward Keona's small house. But

his wife kept looking back to their hut as if she were afraid to leave it.

"You *should* worry," I muttered. "Because I know you're leaving and I may destroy your little home." I stood then and started down the side of the crater, keeping my eyes always on Kamaka and his white horse.

I held my head high and stalked past his partially built house without stopping. I would prefer to leave the potato there for the woman to find later. But Boki had ordered me to deliver it in person.

"I want to know exactly what she does when you give it," he'd said. "Don't miss a detail."

"Why?" I had asked. "Why give your enemy a sweet potato?"

"Because," said Boki, "Malia was my woman, and I will *never* let her forget it. When she was mine, I supplied her with sweet potatoes." He rubbed his hands together with enthusiasm. "And now," he said, "I see I gave her leprosy, too."

I followed Pele, Kamaka, and his wife at a distance, stopping when they arrived at Keona's grass hut. I pressed myself behind a large boulder and peeked over the edge to keep an eye on Kamaka.

He helped his wife dismount and talked to Keona at the door of her hut. Then he turned Pele's head and came in my direction.

I ducked. I slithered around the side of the boulder and waited. From the sound of Pele's hooves, I knew Kamaka would pass me on the *makai* side of the boulder, the one that faced the sea. I inched my way around the other side of the large stone.

Within minutes Kamaka was gone. I flattened myself to the ground and waited. When I peered out again, Pele and Kamaka were headed out toward the valley that cut into the cliffs of Moloka'i.

When he was out of sight, I stood and walked boldly toward Keona's hut.

It would be easier if Keona had not befriended Kamaka and his wife. I did not want to feel her disappointment in me. But even so, I felt safe in delivering a simple sweet potato. Surely Keona would not guess the malice behind Boki's gift.

Maka Nui saw me coming and ran to greet me. "Pia," she said when she saw the food in my hand, "did you bring me a sweet potato?"

I wished the potato *were* for Maka Nui. Things would be so much easier if I could simply give kindness and not pain.

But then I remembered that it was anger and not kindness that had helped me survive in this place. I pushed back feelings of regret and pulled up the anger again. *After all,* I thought, *where was Kamaka when I was hungry and scared?*

I punched Maka Nui playfully on the shoulder. "I'm sorry," I said. "The potato is for your new friend. It's a gift from Boki."

As we neared the house, I saw that Keona sat with Malia on a mat by the door of the hut. Malia was just beginning to weave a mat of her own. I heard her talking as Maka Nui and I walked up.

I put my hand on Maka Nui's shoulder. "Shh," I whispered. "Let's surprise them!" I stopped and listened to their conversation.

"Kamaka is gathering more *hala* leaves for me now," said the younger woman. "We need more mats. The ground is so damp here."

"You are fortunate, Malia," Keona said. "Many women don't have the care of a strong husband when they come to Moloka'i."

"They almost didn't let him come," said Malia. "There's a new law about bringing family. 'No helpers,' the sheriff said.

But I pleaded with him, and he made arrangements for Kamaka to work here as a constable."

Kamaka, a constable? I nearly smashed the sweet potato in my anger. Did he think he was going to be in charge here?

Keona looked up then and saw me there with Maka Nui. She smiled and her whole face went bright. "*Aloha* to you, Pia. What mischief are you up to today?"

"*Aloha* to you," I replied. "I have a gift for your new neighbor." I hoped Keona didn't see the awkwardness I felt. I heard my voice quiver. "We thought you might be hungry," I said, pressing the potato into Malia's hand. "Boki sent it."

I felt the jolt when Malia jerked herself away. She dropped the sweet potato. "No!" she gasped. "I don't want it."

There was a rustling behind me and then a voice, harsh and demanding. "What's going on? What are you doing to my wife?"

Kamaka! How did he sneak up on me? I thought I'd been so careful.

I heard Kamaka slide off Pele. I felt Pele nudge my shoulder in recognition. I wanted to greet her, too, but I made myself ignore her.

Kamaka strode past me and put his arm around his wife. I hated him for that. Where had he been when *I* needed a protector?

I tossed my head defiantly. "I was only delivering a gift," I said. "I didn't mean to scare her."

"Look, Kamaka," said Maka Nui. "It's a sweet potato. Boki sent it." Maka Nui held the potato up for Kamaka to see.

"Boki!" snarled Kamaka. He snatched the potato from Maka Nui's hand and hurled it toward the *pali*.

Maka Nui gasped. "But, but—I'm hungry."

Kamaka looked at the child and his expression did not

soften. "If you're hungry, *I* will bring you food," he said. "Never take anything from Boki's hand."

He turned to me. "I'm disappointed in you, Pia. I thought you would use better judgment in choosing your friends."

I looked at Kamaka. Who was *he* to talk of friendship? Who was *he* to be disappointed in *me*?

"Yes," I said. "You would think so, wouldn't you? But I chose you, didn't I?" Then I turned and stalked away.

"Wait, Pia!" I heard Kamaka behind me. I felt his touch on my arm, and then he turned me around to face him. I jerked myself free.

"Don't touch! I have leprosy now. Remember?"

Kamaka's head went down. "Pia," he pleaded. "Let me explain."

I thought then about my dream and how Kamaka wanted to go for a swim. How I'd poured my buckets of water on the ground and declared I'd never swim with him again.

It was just a dream.

But thinking about it gave me courage. And remembering my time in Kalihi Hospital did too. I'd waited for an explanation and Kamaka had not come. I'd been in this settlement for four years and he hadn't sent a single word of greeting.

Now he stood before me, stammering for words. I tossed them back in his face. "No, Kamaka. The time for explaining is past."

I turned and nearly ran back to Boki's house. I couldn't wait to tell him how his sweet potato had upset Kamaka and Malia.

19

Ka Hoʻomaʻalea
[TO TRICK]

The next Friday, when Boki sent me to deliver his sweet potato, I wrapped it in a *kī* leaf and set out on the dusty path that led toward the center of the peninsula.

When I came to the worn trail that led to Keona's house, I gave three long whistles and two short ones. Within moments Maka Nui came around a bend in the trail.

She laughed when she saw me and I smiled at the sight of her. But she was so thin. I thought that at eight years old she should be bigger. I wished she could get more food. And I wished I could take her away from here. The leprosy settlement was no place for a child to grow up. *If* she grew up ...

Maka Nui was one of those people who didn't show much sign of our disease. Her face was still clear, and her hands and feet were too. But I knew the doctors must have found some spots somewhere under that long dress she wore.

She ran to me now, her hands extended. "Did you bring it?" she squealed.

"Shhh, this potato is a secret, remember? You can't tell anyone. Not even Keona."

I stamped on the grasses to make a path to a low rock wall that ran nearby. I picked Maka Nui up and set her on the stones. Then I handed her the sweet potato.

She held its warmth to her cheek. Her face was streaked with dirt and layered with a smile. "Mmmmm," she said. She closed her eyes and inhaled. "I'm almost afraid to eat it. Because then I won't have it anymore."

"Just remember," I said, "next Friday there will be another one. I'll bring the biggest one in Boki's basket."

Maka Nui giggled. "Praise be to the Lord," she said.

"You sound just like Keona." I leaned back against the rock wall and hoisted myself up beside my little friend. I was relieved that I'd thought of a way to deliver Boki's potatoes without angering Kamaka or upsetting his wife. But mostly I was glad that I could give Maka Nui something she truly needed.

She took a big bite. "Why doesn't Malia want Boki's potatoes? Isn't she hungry?"

"I'm sure she's hungry," I said. "But I guess they make her sad."

"But how can potatoes make you sad?"

"I don't know. Maybe they're a memory of something bad."

Maka Nui took another bite of the potato and said with her mouth full, "Good memories can make you sad, too. I'm sad when I think of my family."

I hadn't thought much about Maka Nui's life before Kalawao. "What do you remember?" I asked.

"I remember eating *poi* every day." Maka Nui scooped three fingers into the center of the sweet potato and brought its flesh up to her mouth. "Mmmmm," she said as she licked delicious bits of potato from her fingertips. "And I remember catching shrimps with my father. What do you remember?"

"I remember Yellow Cat snuggling with me at night and waking me up in the morning. I remember walking to school and wishing I could go surf-riding instead."

Maka Nui leaned her head against my shoulder. "I remember my mother singing to me when I had bad dreams." She stared at the white cloud puffs that floated in the perfect blue sky. "But I can't remember what my mother looks like. Do you remember what your mother looks like?"

I stared into the clouds too, but I couldn't bring back the sunny look of my mother's face. Then I thought about Kimi. "I remember how my little sister looked," I said. "She looked like you."

"Really?" Maka Nui gripped my shoulder and pulled herself up until she was standing on the rock wall. She stuffed the last of the potato into her mouth and turned to face me. "Is that why you're nice to me, Pia? Why aren't you nice to anyone else?"

I looked at my little friend and thought that she was too smart. "I'm nice to Keona," I said. "Two friends are enough."

I stood on the wall and started walking toward the sea. A field mouse peeked its head from between some stones and scuttled along the wall in front of me.

I heard Maka Nui's voice following me. "What about Boki? Is he your friend?"

"No!" I called back.

"Do you hate Boki?"

I turned to face her. I put one cautious foot behind the other as I walked backward along the low wall. It wasn't easy because the rocks were loosely stacked and sometimes one would clatter to the ground. I had to be careful or I would fall.

I watched Maka Nui balance herself, arms outstretched. There was a long tear under the sleeve of her brown dress so that now I could see the marks of leprosy in her armpit. Behind her, I saw the great green cliffs of Moloka'i—our prison walls.

"Of course I hate Boki. Everybody hates Boki," I said.

"Then why do you live with him?"

"Because my family isn't here. Keona adopted you, and Boki adopted me. If I leave, he will kill me."

"You could live with Kamaka and Malia. Kamaka is a constable. He wouldn't let Boki kill you."

I turned around again and walked with my back to Maka Nui. I fastened my eye on the ocean. "Let's see how far we can go on the walls," I yelled. I picked up my pace and spread my arms.

"Can I go first?"

I stopped and waited for Maka Nui to squeeze past me. She led the way along the wall, her body tipping this way and that as she balanced herself.

When the wall came to an intersection, she looked both ways and then turned toward the Kauhakō Crater. Ahead of us I saw Kamaka's house. I waited to see if Maka Nui would turn away when the wall intersected with another one, but she kept going straight—toward the place where Kamaka and Malia lived.

I followed her until I was close enough to the house to see that no one was there. Then I jumped down and said, "I have to go now. I have work to do for Boki." I took Maka Nui's hand and turned her around. I walked with her—she was on the wall and I was on the ground—until I saw Keona's shack. Then I lifted her down and said, "Go find Keona. She's probably worried about you."

Maka Nui ran toward her home. Then she stopped and turned around. "I liked the sweet potato!" she called.

"Shhh!" I warned her.

But I doubted that our secret would be ours alone for long. Ah Loy was probably lurking inside the tall grasses that very minute.

When I saw Maka Nui go inside Keona's house, I turned and headed for Kamaka's place. I looked all around me as I walked, keeping my eyes open for the sight of Pele. As I got closer to Kamaka's shelter, I ducked and crawled along the rock wall.

When I came to the section of wall that enclosed the shelter, I heard the grunting of a wild pig.

I peered over the stones and saw that Kamaka had used tree branches to pen the pig. Nearby was a hole in the ground, lined with rocks.

Of course! Kamaka was preparing to roast the pig.

A picture floated across my mind—steam wafting, the smell of roast pork, fingers dipping into a calabash of *poi*. Kamaka eating with my family.

I could almost hear my mother's voice. Telling again the story of me as a baby. Of Kamaka's first visit—how they'd dragged him in to greet me. How he'd crossed his arms on his chest and grumbled an *aloha*. How that was the moment when our friendship began. And how it had always been there.

At least until I got leprosy.

The thought of Kamaka's rejection made me hate that pig. I did not want to smell it cooking when I rode across the peninsula. And I didn't want Kamaka to enjoy a feast without me.

I leaped across the rock wall and kicked at the sticks that formed Kamaka's pig pen. I tore at them with my hands and flung them into the grass outside Kamaka's stone enclosure.

And when the pig ran grunting through the opening and out onto the peninsula, I laughed. That would show Kamaka how wrong he'd been!

Then I turned and leaped over the wall again. And when I did, I realized I'd been caught.

Malia stood there, her hand over her mouth, tears in her eyes. "Why?" she whispered. "Pia, why do you hate us so much?"

20

Ka Hilahila

[ASHAMED]

I landed with a jolt, and when I put out a hand to balance myself, Malia caught it. She didn't let go but looked intently into my face. "Pia, what have we done to make you so angry?"

I couldn't look at her anymore, so I stared at the ground. I dug my toes around a coarse lava pebble. *If only I could skitter sideways like a crab beneath the tunnels in the grass. Or dart like a mongoose along the low edge of the rock wall—away from Kamaka's home. If only I could put the pig back where I found it.*

I looked around for Kamaka but did not see him.

"Kamaka is not here," said Malia. "He's making a delivery to Mr. Meyer." She pointed to the cliffs.

I looked toward the top of the *pali.* But I wasn't thinking about Mr. Meyer. I was thinking about Kamaka climbing the *pali* trail. I knew how dangerous it was, steep and slippery in some spots and completely washed out in others.

Malia gripped my arm. "Do you think Kamaka will come back safely?"

"Don't worry," I said. "If *he* can't climb the *pali,* no one can. Even Mr. Meyer comes over the trail sometimes."

Malia sighed with relief. "Kamaka wants to buy food up there. It's too soon for our garden to produce. And anyway," she said, "someone keeps pulling up our plants."

I was looking down now, but I felt her watching me. I was

sure she could see that I was the one who'd been there just a few days earlier.

When I dared lift my head I saw those dry patches of leprosy along her neck.

I wished I hadn't seen them again. I didn't like how they connected her to me.

"You didn't tell me why you hate us so much," said Malia. "Sit down. I will make you coffee."

"No!" I said. When I saw the hurt in her eyes, I softened my tone. "I mean—I'll sit. But I don't want to use up all your coffee. Keep it for yourselves."

I sat on the rock wall and watched as she scrambled over it into the enclosure that surrounded her home. Slowly I turned and swung my legs over the wall so that I was included in the little corral. I felt strange, at home but out of place—almost hugged by this shelter I'd been trying to destroy. I slid to the ground and leaned back against the rocks. I pulled my legs up to my chin and huddled there. Something about this quiet woman pulled me into her enclosure.

Malia sat on a stone in front of me and asked me again, "Why do you hate us?"

"I don't hate *you*," I said. "It's Kamaka I hate."

"But why? I thought you and Kamaka were friends."

I snorted softly. "I thought so, too."

"What happened?"

I looked at her in surprise. I had assumed she knew everything. But then again, maybe I wasn't important enough for Kamaka to mention to his wife.

"Kamaka came to my house when I was born," I said. "Our mothers say we loved each other from the beginning."

I hadn't intended to say so much. But now that I'd started, the story tumbled out. "I ate my first *poi* from Kamaka's finger.

He taught me to walk and I followed him everywhere. I started my life with him and I thought he would be there to the end."

"What happened?"

I didn't want to repeat the story of Kamaka's rejection. "Why don't you ask him?"

"I did," said Malia. "But he won't talk about it. Kamaka is strong on the outside. But inside he carries a shame that he has never shared with me."

Malia's words reminded me of something my mother had said when she came to see me in the hospital. She told me that Kamaka was too ashamed to visit me. Tūtū had also talked of shame. *Kamaka was once a child*, too, she'd told me. I remembered the sadness on her face when she said it. And how her voice faded to a whisper.

"When did you stop being friends?" asked Malia.

I wondered the same thing. *When did we stop being friends? And why? Why, after always being there, did Kamaka disappear one day and not come back?* I reached for one of the sticks I'd taken from the pigpen. I peeled at its bark while I struggled with the questions.

"At first when I got leprosy, I thought he would rescue me. Kamaka knows about plants and medicines. I thought he would know some bark to boil for tea or a plant to make into a poultice for my sores." I tossed a bit of bark over Malia's head and watched it disappear with the wind. "But he didn't come to my house with a remedy."

Malia gripped the other end of the stick. "So then the Board of Health brought you here?"

"First they took me to Kalihi Hospital. I waited for Kamaka to visit. But he never came. And when they sent me to Moloka'i he did not come to the wharf to give me his *aloha*."

I leaned my head against the wall and closed my eyes so

I would not see Malia looking into my pain. But I heard her voice, and it was gentle and sad.

"Kamaka is afraid of leprosy," she said. "I saw his face when I showed him my spots the first time. I felt him pull away from me. He even ran from me. But I think he's trying to conquer his fear. He wants to put things right."

I didn't say anything. I stared past Malia's head and sat with her in silence as the sun crept off past the landing place and along the western sea cliffs of Moloka'i.

Eventually Malia tugged gently on the stick we held between us. "He wants to be your friend, Pia. Give him another chance."

I thought that it was easy for Malia to trust Kamaka. But she did not know how it felt to come here alone. Perhaps she *had* seen fear on Kamaka's face when he learned about her illness. Whatever Kamaka felt—at least Malia had seen it.

When *I* got leprosy, he did not see my spots. And I did not see his fear. He simply disappeared. And I had almost gotten used to it.

Now my eye caught a movement in the distance, on the *pali* that towered above us. A man was coming down the trail.

"Kamaka is coming," I said. I began to rebuild the wooden pen I'd destroyed. I retrieved the sticks I'd thrown in anger. I worked silently, carefully, until the broken wall was rebuilt. "I will return the things I stole from you," I promised.

Then I leaped over the wall and ran across the plain. I did not look back.

21

Ke Kaumaha

[SORROW]

I wanted to return all of Malia's possessions. But Boki had most of her books, and he intended to keep them for himself. He'd already traded some of the other items for favors from his neighbors.

At least I could return her catechism. I decided to do it one afternoon when Boki was sleeping in the next room.

I slipped Malia's book from beneath my mattress. I opened the book and turned its pages. It had the Ten Commandments written there. I'd learned those from the Protestants in Honolulu. And I had broken many of them since coming to this place. Especially the one about stealing.

The Apostles' Creed was there, too. I looked down through the statements it made about our Lord, "… was crucified, died, and was buried. He descended into hell …" I turned the pages and saw some prayers: "Our Father who art in heaven …"

So where is God? I wondered. *In heaven or in hell?*

I thought about Keona and her Protestant church friends. To me their God seemed far away from this place, but they loved Him and trusted Him to help them.

And now here was Malia, who had brought a Catholic book with her. I'd seen her going with other Catholics into Saint Philomena's Church, the one built by Brother Bertrant. But since there was no priest here to conduct services, Malia was probably desperate for this book.

I tucked it into the waist of my trousers. Satisfied with the level of Boki's snoring, I tiptoed outside and across the yard. I climbed onto Māui and turned him toward the center of the peninsula. I would ride out toward Kamaka's homestead to see if Pele was tied there. If not, I would take the book to Malia.

Ahead, I saw two men on the trail. Between them they carried an old blanket with a long lump wrapped inside.

Another death.

I slowed Māui when I came alongside them. I recognized Hulu, the quiet man who had come on the ship with me. He stared straight ahead, saying nothing.

But the other man offered an explanation. "He has gone on the road of no return."

"Your 'ohana?" I asked.

The man shook his head. "No," he said. "But he died near my clump of grass. We must move him."

"Where will you bury him?" I asked.

The man nodded toward Kauhakō. "We will throw him in the crater."

I nodded and urged Māui forward.

Someone died nearly every day on the peninsula. If they were lucky, friends would dig a shallow grave. But tools and the strength to use them were scarce in Kalawao.

I worried how it would feel to die. But mostly I worried if anyone would even care. Would Boki kick me into a shallow ditch for the pigs to eat? Would Kamaka throw my body in the crater? Would anyone even know?

Out ahead on the trail, I saw a horse and rider coming toward me. Pele and Kamaka!

I could turn around so that I wouldn't have to meet Kamaka. But where would I go? Even if I avoided him now, I could not do it forever. He had followed me to this island, and I couldn't get away from him.

Māui nickered softly and trotted faster toward Pele. I looked straight ahead as we came closer.

Kamaka reined Pele to a stop.

I dug my knees into Māui's side, but he paid no attention. Instead, he slowed down to greet Pele and put his nose to hers. I jerked on the reins, but Māui did not pull away. He took a step closer, stretching to scratch Pele's neck with his teeth. The sharp, familiar scent of the two sweaty horses filled me with memories.

I yanked the reins, but Māui pushed into Pele, scratching her hide. And Pele scratched back.

Even when I slapped Māui with the reins, he only sidestepped. Pele followed, and the two of them performed a sort of dance on the rocky trail. Māui nickered softly. His voice was a pleading that made my throat ache.

"At least *they* haven't forgotten each other." Kamaka's voice was sad and accusing. I felt his eyes inviting me, but I turned my head.

He did not look like the old Kamaka anyway—not with the light gone from his eyes. And he was so quiet. Without his laughter, Kamaka was a stranger.

I kicked Māui sharply. He lurched forward but trotted only a short distance before stopping again.

Kamaka's voice called back to me, "We could be friends, too."

I kicked Māui again. I smacked him with the reins and slapped him with my hands. He galloped across the peninsula. From behind us I heard the high sound of Pele's whinny. Māui called back.

I rode fast but I did not turn on the trail that led to Kamaka and Malia's house. Suddenly I didn't want to see Malia after all.

I galloped back and forth across the plain, jumping low

rock walls and dashing around boulders. But wherever I rode I couldn't get far enough away from Kamaka and Pele. From Kalawao and leprosy.

I felt again how I was trapped here.

I rode out to the sea and sat by its edge while Māui rested. I imagined I saw the faint outline of Diamond Head in the distance. I saw the sunlight playing on its red sides and the blue cloud shadows that chased after the sun.

I didn't think it was real. Surely I could *not* see Diamond Head from this distance. But many times I had sat on this black shoreline and looked out over the water. In my mind I had seen so much of my home from this spot.

I had seen my mother and Kimi heading to the market, loaded down with flower garlands they'd made to sell. And coming home with trinkets and necessaries they'd gotten in exchange.

I'd seen Kimi's face pleading with me to play with her. If I could be there again—at home on Waikiki—I would swim with her instead of pushing her aside to follow Kamaka into the surf.

But I would never see Kimi again, never sleep in my mother's house, never again eat *poi* with Kamaka, Lani, and Tūtū.

This peninsula was my world now. It was all that I ever saw. And it was so desolate.

Where were its banana and orange trees? Its curved palms and straight papayas? What had this place been like before the coming of leprosy? Had there ever been trees in Kalawao?

I supposed they'd been cut down by the first patients seven years earlier. How else could they have built their shelters? Now the only tree left in the settlement was that small *hala* tree beside the Catholic church. I had to wonder if it had been left for some special purpose.

Why was it still growing in this graveyard?

I had so many questions …

Later I turned back toward the Kauhakō Crater. When I rode close to Kamaka's home, I saw that no one was there. So I hopped down from Māui and pulled the prayer book from my waistband. I placed it in a metal pot just inside the door.

I could have looked to see what kind of home Kamaka had made for Malia. I could have peered into the life they made together there. But I didn't. I turned instead, climbed on my horse, and rode away—back into the cold winds of Kalawao.

22

Ke Kamaʻilio

[TO CONVERSE]

"Pia. Where are you?" The voice of Ah Loy awakened me from an afternoon sleep.

I rubbed my eyes and considered ignoring his call. But Ah Loy was persistent. Through the window I saw him hopping impatiently from one foot to the other. I knew he would not go away, so I got up and went outside.

"The woman," said Ah Loy. "She wants to see you."

"Keona? Is she in trouble? Is Maka Nui sick?"

"Not the old woman. Malia, the wife of the constable. She said to come now."

I was confused. Malia was not the kind of woman who ordered others around.

Ah Loy did not wait for me to ask questions. "I am telling you the truth," he said.

I began walking toward Malia's house, but when I heard Ah Loy following me, I decided to take Māui instead.

"I could ride behind you," said Ah Loy.

"I don't need your help."

"But I brought you this message," he said. "So let me ride your horse."

I knew Ah Loy was only curious about what Malia wanted. "Well," I said to myself, "Ah Loy does not need to know everything. And the rest of the settlement doesn't either."

I put my left foot into the stirrup and brought my right one over Māui's hind parts. I settled into the saddle and gave Ah Loy a nod as I flicked the reins.

"I had a horse, too," Ah Loy called after me.

"In Hawai'i, everyone has a horse," I said. "But you do not have one on Moloka'i, do you?" For a moment I enjoyed having something that Ah Loy wanted. But the pleasure of it turned sour as I thought of him standing there watching me ride away like a selfish *haole*. I had become a foreigner myself since coming to Moloka'i—someone I did not understand.

But of course, this settlement was like a foreign land.

Ahead of me in the grass, near Keona's hut, I saw Malia. She waved and ran to meet me. I slapped the reins lightly and let Māui amble through the coarse grasses with their waving seed heads. When I came to a rock wall, I stopped and waited for Malia. I saw that she carried a small object in her hand. It was the Catholic book I'd given back to her.

Malia leaned over the wall and grabbed Māui's reins. "Oh, Pia. I had to tell you. When I realized my book was gone I thought God had left me. When you brought it back, I knew He was here after all!"

"I wish I could get the other books for you, but Boki has them."

"Don't worry about it," said Malia. "Books would make the days go better, but at least my family sends newspapers. And my catechism—I missed it most."

She pulled the book to herself. She put her face into its open pages and closed her eyes. She was like a hungry little girl inhaling the scent of a roasted sweet potato.

How could this book mean so much?

"I looked at the book," I said. "I don't see why it's so good."

"Oh, I'll show you," said Malia. "Listen!" She opened the

book and searched for a passage. "Here it is!" She read softly as if God himself were listening.

"Our Father who art in heaven,
Hallowed be thy name.
Thy Kingdom come,
Thy will be done on earth
As it is in heaven."

I had learned the same prayer in my Protestant church. But it didn't comfort me here on Moloka'i.

Malia continued reading.

"Give us this day our daily bread."

What good did it do to ask for bread in Kalawao? If the Christians in this place were getting their prayers answered, I could not see it. They were as hungry as the rest of us.

"And forgive us our trespasses
As we forgive those who trespass against us."

Forgive? I did not want to forgive. And I did not much care to be forgiven.

Malia paused to look at me. I suppose she could see that her book did not comfort me. "Pia," she said. "God is all we have left now. He is the only one who will help us here."

I didn't want to argue. So I just said, "Since you like it so much, I'm glad I brought it back."

Malia climbed over the rock wall and sat down to explain. "When I got leprosy I was terrified. I knew I would have to leave my family. I knew Kamaka was afraid of my disease. Then Kamiano gave me this book and it said what I felt. Listen."

She searched through her book for some other precious words, but the breeze tossed the pages one way as Malia turned them the other. She brushed strands of her long hair away from her face.

I wasn't sure I wanted to hear more of her book, so I tried to distract her. "Who is Kamiano?" I asked.

Malia stopped her searching. "Kamiano," she whispered and her deep brown eyes went bright. "Makua Kamiano is a priest in Kohala. His *haole* name is Father Damien. He is the one who brought God's *aloha* to me."

Father Damien? I was sure this was the priest that Boki had talked about. He had said his mother loved the priest like he was part of her *'ohana*.

But *I* had no fondness for a Catholic priest.

"Oh," I said. "A priest? And how did he give you God's *aloha*?"

Malia held the book close as if she thought God's love was kept between its covers. "Kamiano showed me what God's love is like," she said. "He left his home across the ocean to live among us. Just as we are cut off from our families, he is separated from his."

I shrugged. What did I care about this Kamiano choosing to leave his family? As far as I was concerned, he could go back to where he came from. "Strangers from all over the world choose to come here," I said. "In Hawai'i the scenery is so splendid and fish and fruit are so plentiful that they don't want to leave again. Is this such a sacrifice for your priest?"

Malia nodded. "Yes, it is, Pia. Kamiano does not live a life of ease. Every day he works hard, building churches and teaching us about God. He climbs up and down our *pali* walls and crosses dangerous waters to reach our people."

I thought about the words in Malia's book, about our Lord descending into hell.

"Oh," I said. "But he would never descend the *pali* here."

I pointed to the green cliffs that rose above us, separating our peninsula from the rest of Molokaʻi island. "Kamiano would not cross the stormy waters off Kalawao. He would not bring God's *aloha* to this place, would he?"

"Pia, many people depend on Kamiano. He couldn't just leave them to come here."

"Of course not," I said. "Your Catholics send a priest for short visits, and the Reverend Forbes visits the Church of the Healing Spring. But no healthy minister will come here to live. Not even your Father in heaven could live here."

Malia sighed. "You are like Kamaka," she said.

"No!" I argued. I dug my knees into Māui's side, and my startled horse began to back away from the rock wall. "I am *not* like Kamaka." I blocked out the image of my younger self—swimming in the ocean, climbing on the mountains, straining to be just like him.

Instead, I thought of other memories—of me waiting in the hospital, of Kamaka watching from the top of Diamond Head while the steamer hauled me away.

"I will never be like Kamaka!" I declared.

"Yes," said Malia sadly. "You *are* like Kamaka. You speak of God as my God—as if you do not believe in Him—but still you are angry with Him. The cliffs of Molokaʻi are not your prison, Pia. Your anger is your prison."

I liked Malia, but not when she talked like this.

If anger was my prison, I welcomed its walls. My anger made me alert. It kept me from expecting things and being disappointed when they didn't happen.

I would not stop being angry. I would not let Kamaka sneak back into my life.

I turned to Malia. "I will be *your* friend, Malia, but don't expect me to forgive Kamaka." Then I backed Māui away from the rock wall and turned him toward the trail that ran along the cliffs of Moloka'i.

But Malia's words about God's love followed me. And I couldn't get the name of her priest out of my head. Makua Kamiano—Father Damien—Makua Kamiano …

23

Ka Pōpoki

[CAT]

I was used to finding stray dogs and wild pigs on Boki's lanai. They often rooted around the yard in search of food. But I did not expect to find a kitten on the porch. Especially not in an old cloth bag.

I knew it was a kitten before I opened the bag. And I knew someone had delivered it in the darkness of early morning. I'd heard the footsteps, but by the time I got to the window, the intruder was gone.

I saw a strange lump moving on the floor of the porch and went out to investigate.

The kitten meowed loudly before I opened the bag and hissed at me when I reached my hand inside. I jerked my hand back. "Don't be afraid," I said softly. "I'm not going to hurt you." I sat on the porch floor and pulled the bundle onto my lap, against my belly. I stayed like that for a long time.

"Where did you come from, little *pōpoki*?" I asked. "Did you ask to live with me? Do you know how mean Boki is? Stay out of his way or he may kick you from here to the top of the *pali*."

In this way I made friends with the kitten before I ever saw it. And by the time daylight came and I reached into the bag to bring it out, it was too late to reject it.

When I saw its yellow color I was both thrilled and angry—thrilled because for one moment it seemed to be my own Yellow Cat yawning in my lap, but angry because I knew it was Kamaka who had brought him. Besides Maka Nui, he was the only one who knew about Yellow Cat.

I did not want to receive any gift from Kamaka's hand.

When Boki saw the kitten, he threatened to drown him. "I hate cats!" he said. "And I won't have that pile of yellow bones eating my tinned salmon."

I cradled Pōpoki against my chest. "He won't touch your food," I promised. "There are lots of mice living in these rock walls and stealing your rice in the cookhouse. We need a cat to protect your supplies."

"If I ever catch him, I'll wring his neck."

In spite of his threats, I felt sure I'd convinced Boki that a cat would be valuable. Still, I didn't take any chances. When I went out, I always took the kitten with me.

I couldn't wait to see Maka Nui's face when she saw him.

She met me that Friday at the usual intersection in the rock walls. I handed her the sweet potato. While she ate, I stroked Pōpoki, who was tucked beneath my shirt. "Shhh," I whispered when he meowed softly.

"What was that?" asked Maka Nui. She stood with one hand gripping her precious potato and the other on her hip. "What do you have, Pia?"

"Oh, nothing. Just another sweet potato. Boki was feeling generous this week."

"No. Boki never feels generous. I heard something and it wasn't a sweet potato."

The kitten meowed again, and this time Maka Nui knew what it was. She clapped her hand over her surprised mouth. "A cat? Do you have a cat?"

I reached inside my shirt and brought Pōpoki out. "He came to my house," I said. "While I was sleeping, he came to Boki's *lānai* and woke me up."

Maka Nui reached for the cat. "It's your Yellow Cat, Pia. But how did he come?"

"It's not the same one," I said. "I heard someone bring this kitten to the porch. I think it was Kamaka."

"Can I hold him?"

I hesitated. What if the kitten slipped from her hands and ran away?

"Finish your potato first," I said.

Maka Nui stuffed the rest of the potato in her mouth. She gulped it down so fast I thought it would choke her.

I laughed. "Be careful. The kitten will still be here when you're finished." Then I handed him to her.

"Oh, Pia. Aren't you so happy?" Maka Nui brushed the kitten's nose against her own.

I thought about her question. I was glad that I could bring Maka Nui a few small pleasures in this place. But for myself, I wasn't sure I remembered how happy felt.

Even the kitten produced a mix of feelings. I did not want to keep him, and yet I could not let him go.

Kamaka knew I wouldn't take the kitten from his hand. So, like a thief in the darkness, he slipped Pōpoki to me. I didn't like how Kamaka gave me things I couldn't get for myself. First he had sent Māui, and now here was Pōpoki.

Thinking about Kamaka made me feel restless.

"I have to go," I said. "Boki always waits for a report on how Malia liked the potato."

Maka Nui giggled. "And what do you tell him?" she asked.

"I tell him Malia drops it on the ground. Sometimes I tell him she throws it back at me and begs me to stop torturing her. I tell him she weeps at the mention of his name."

"And then what does Boki do?" asked Maka Nui.

"He smiles so big and so wicked I can see how many teeth

he is missing. He tells me to take her a bigger one next Friday." I climbed onto Māui's back and reached for the kitten. "I'll bring him back another day," I said.

When I reached the road that ran through Kalawao, I saw Ah Loy talking to Boki on his porch.

"What is Ah Loy up to now?" I asked myself. "This cannot be good."

I met him on the road just outside Boki's yard. I stopped to see if he had some news for me also. "*Aloha* to you," said Ah Loy, continuing on his way.

I did not return his greeting.

Boki was on the porch waiting for my report. He tapped his foot impatiently while I dismounted and tied Māui to his post. "What did she do when you gave her the potato?" he demanded.

I cuddled Pōpoki and spun a tale. "She trembled," I said.

Boki grinned wickedly. His failing eye glittered. "Trembled," he said. "How did she tremble?"

"First it was her lips that quivered," I said. "I thought she was going to cry, but she didn't. I thought she was going to ask me why I keep bringing potatoes, but she didn't."

"What *did* she do?"

"Her hands began to shake. Then her whole body shook."

"Good," said Boki. "I hope she quivered like a dry seed pod in the wind."

"She did," I said. "I could hear her teeth clattering." I stroked Pōpoki while I tried to think of a new twist to the familiar story.

Boki seemed especially impatient for details. "And then what?" he snapped.

"And then she reached for the potato. She pressed her thumbs into its soft flesh and said, 'These are Boki's eyes.'"

"Oh, is that what she said?" Boki was enjoying the story more than usual. "And what new threat has she come up with?" he asked.

"She smashed it on a rock. She said, 'Tell Boki this is what will happen to him if he sends any more potatoes.'"

Boki's eyes narrowed. He stepped off the porch and leaned into my face. He was so close I could count the few remaining hairs in his one eyebrow. I turned my head to avoid the foulness of his breath.

I thought Boki was going to shout some new message for Malia. But his anger was not for her.

"Liar! You did not give the potato to Malia. You have not given any of them to her! You tricked me, Pia. I have a witness! And you will not get away with it."

I felt the wrenching as Boki grabbed Pōpoki. But I did not expect what happened next. I lunged for my cat but lost my balance and fell across the porch floor. Above me, I heard Pōpoki scream as Boki twisted her neck.

I scrambled to my feet in time to see Boki throw Pōpoki's limp body across the stone wall that surrounded his house.

I was on top of Boki then. I shoved him to the floor. "You killed my cat!" I screamed. "You killed my cat! I'll kill you, Boki!" I smashed my fist into his face. He twisted his head to avoid the blows, but there was no escaping my revenge.

Again and again I hit the man who had entrapped me. I did not think of the moment that I realized I was trapped. I did not think about the hard work I'd done for the last four years, or the cruelties that Boki had inflicted on me. I did not think at all. I simply released the anger that had collected. Anger toward Boki, toward Kamaka, and even toward God.

"Stop it, Pia!" I felt a strong hand on my shoulder. I recognized the voice and felt Kamaka pulling me off Boki.

I turned to face my other enemy. "Boki killed my cat!" I screamed. Now I hit Kamaka with my anger, pounding my fist into his jaw. He staggered backward. "Why did you bring Pōpoki here?" I shouted.

Kamaka regained his balance and steadied himself. When I thrust another fist at him, he caught my hands and held me off. I twisted out of his grip and turned away. I did not want to see Kamaka's face. I did not want Kamaka to see mine.

I saw Boki cowering on the floor of the porch, groaning curses and meaningless threats. I looked at him lying there helplessly and decided I would never be Boki's boy again. I had outgrown his threats.

"I'm leaving," I announced. "You can send the whole settlement after me if you want. But I'll never work for you again."

I didn't know where I would go, but it hardly mattered.

"Get your things," said Kamaka. "You're coming with me."

"No!" I said. "I do what *I* decide now." I walked toward Māui. I heard Kamaka's footsteps grinding on the loose stones of the yard and felt his hand on my shoulder. I saw the peninsula spin as he whirled me around.

"It's time to forget your anger, Pia. You can't survive alone in this place."

"Alone is better than with a traitor!" I shouted. I saw Kamaka flinch. *Good,* I thought. *You may be stronger than I am. But I can still hurt you.*

"If you don't get your possessions, I will," said Kamaka. His voice was as cold as a Kalawao morning. "And get my things, too, while you're at it. The books you stole and anything else you still have."

I did not move. I looked at Kamaka. I was tired of being afraid of people I didn't like. I didn't want to run away from them. But I didn't want Kamaka to think I needed him, either.

Boldly I looked into his eyes—those familiar brown eyes that used to squint nearly shut when he laughed and dance when he challenged me to a difficult task. I felt him challenging me now.

But his eyes were not dancing.

Kamaka did not blink or look away as he returned my gaze, but I thought his eyelids drooped just a bit. And then he surprised me. "Pia," he said. "I was wrong to leave you when you got leprosy. But I am here now. And you are wrong to hate me this way."

I couldn't look at him anymore. So I looked at my feet instead. A wasp dragged the body of a dead beetle across my blackened toenail. *Yes,* I thought. *You are here now. But you didn't come for me. You came for Malia.*

I turned to go inside Boki's house for the last time. I would gather my possessions. I would not fight with Kamaka anymore.

24

Ma'i

[SICK]

I moved my possessions to Kamaka's stone enclosure. But I only took items sent by my family and the books I'd taken from Kamaka and Malia. I didn't bring anything else that I'd stolen since coming to Moloka'i.

I knew Boki claimed all of those things as his own. And anyway, I hated stealing. Leaving Boki and the life of a criminal was as refreshing as taking a long drink of cold water.

I discovered I was no longer angry with my fellow sufferers.

But I did not want to stop being angry with Kamaka. I ate food if Malia delivered it but ignored anything Kamaka brought to me. I walked to the stream for water and searched the forest for fruit and nuts for the three of us. But I would not sleep under Kamaka's roof.

One afternoon the sky was covered over with clouds and the ocean was whipped into whitecaps. "Please come in," begged Malia. The wind blew her long hair into her eyes, and she pushed it away so she could see me. "Pia, it's going to storm. You will be soaked."

"Good," I said. "It will save me walking to the stream for a bath." But I almost felt sorry when I looked at Malia's face. I could see the worry in her eyes and I didn't like rejecting her kindness. "Don't worry," I added. "I like being outside. This is where I want to be."

Malia was angry. I could see it in her short, jerky movements as she collected her utensils from the outside cooking area and moved them into the house. She snatched up my bundle of clothing, my letters, and other personal possessions.

"I'm not coming inside," I said.

"I know!" said Malia. "You are too stubborn and stupid. But when the rain stops, you will need dry clothing. I'm taking your things inside, and you will not stop me!"

When the rain came, I huddled on the leeward side of the house and tucked my head between my knees. Before long, rain dripped from every part of me, even my eyelashes. I could hear the water running off my shirt.

Through the grass walls of the hut I heard voices and knew that Malia and Kamaka were awake. I tried not to think about them snuggling in the driest corner of the house. No doubt the water was running in under the mats on their floor. I figured I was nearly as dry as they were.

Somehow I fell asleep.

When I awakened, the sun had not exactly appeared over the peninsula, but daylight had come. I stood and stretched my aching muscles. Or was it my bones that ached? I couldn't tell. Everything ached.

The rain continued for hours. I huddled and waited for the rain to stop and for the wind to calm itself. When Kamaka delivered a *kī* leaf of rice and a cup of hot coffee, I gave him only silence. He set them on the ground next to me. The tin cup of coffee collected rainwater and the rice was soon splashed over with dirt.

"You will be sick!" shouted Kamaka, but his words were nearly snatched away by the wind. He leaned over, his face inches from mine. "And then who will care for you when you have rejected all your friends?"

"Rejection, Kamaka? Friends? I learned from you that I don't need friends."

Kamaka sat on the ground just in front of me, and it was like a shelter had been built for me. I felt less of the wind. Water streamed around him, sending it away from the spot where I sat.

Part of me wanted him to stay there until the storm passed. But another part refused to let him see how I felt.

"Pia, your pride will kill you before sickness has a chance."

"Yes," I said. "Then I will be gone and your life will be good again."

There was a long silence. The only sounds were those of the storm.

Finally Kamaka spoke. "Pia, my life will never be good again." His voice was low and sad. "But it will be better if we can be friends."

I looked at Kamaka then. The sight of him made me ache. His black hair was so wet it hung in tight curls around his ears. The rain trickled from his hair and splashed off his shoulders. It dripped from his eyelids and ran down his nose. His wet face reminded me of swims in the ocean and joyful tumbles into mountain streams.

But we were not playing now.

I was too stubborn to let Kamaka see how his words had touched me. So I crossed my arms in front of my chest to show him I didn't care.

He didn't say any more. The only sound was the sound of water. It was all around us. Plinking into the coffee. Splashing into the puddles we sat in. It went on and on until I thought Kamaka would never leave.

And yet I was afraid that he would.

I stared at the water splashing into the cup. I watched how each new splash pushed brown coffee water over the rim and down onto the ground.

After a long while Kamaka stood. When he did, the storm

raged in my face again. He walked away and the wind and the rain stormed against me. When he paused at the corner of his house, I could feel him staring at me, watching me shiver in the tempest he left behind.

I could even feel how he wanted to pick me up and carry me inside.

If only I were a child again, I thought. *A simple, trusting child who would follow him wherever he went ...*

When he had gone into the house, I rubbed my hands together to keep them warm. I rested my head by the uneaten rice and the cup of watery coffee. The rain plinked into the puddles by my ear.

Sometime later, I went to sleep. While I slept, I began to cough. I struggled to open my eyes and thought I saw sunshine. I begged for water.

I dreamed I was at the top of the Kauhakō Crater. The goddess Pele flamed in my face and sent hot lava through my body. She scorched me with her heat and I could not get away from the burning. I dreamed that Kamaka brought two buckets of water and used one to spoon cool liquids into my mouth. I dreamed that he used water from the other bucket to cool my scorching flesh and that he built a shelter over me to block the burning of the sun.

In my dream he sat with me in that shelter. He laid his head on my chest and begged me to forgive him. "Pia, I was so afraid. I'm sorry. I will never leave you again." Kamaka's sad voice broke my hard heart. His tears cooled my burning flesh.

But, of course, it was only a dream ...

When I awoke, I did not lie in the rain or under the hot sun. I lay on a dry *lau hala* mat and was covered with a light blanket. Overhead I saw a thatched roof that Kamaka must have built while I was sleeping. I was enclosed in my own room with three sides newly built. The other side was the wall of Kamaka's house.

I was too tired to ask questions. I went back to sleep and dreamed that I was growing strong again.

25

Pilikia!

[TROUBLE!]

I dreamed that Kamaka, wanting to put things right between us, took me to visit Kauhakō. In my dream I followed him right to the rim and saw that it was not a dead volcano after all. Red-hot lava boiled up to its edge. A magnificent bubble broke forth and splashed Kamaka so that he was covered with glowing lava drops. But they did not burn him.

Then Boki was there, threatening to push Kamaka into the boiling crater. I wanted to push Boki over the edge, but I was too afraid. He put his face up to mine, and his eyes—both of them—were glowing. His breath singed my hair; the smell of it sickened me.

"You will come with me," he said. "Bring those books you stole." He turned to go as if he was sure I would simply follow him. And then he called over his shoulder, "Oh, and bring that woman too. She was mine first."

He started down a shiny path. That was when I saw he was not alone. A mob was with him.

The mob sounded angry. And Boki's voice was louder than all of the others. "Give me the boy. Give me the books. I want my woman."

I knew this was a dream, so I shook myself to get free of it. But it was not a dream. The angry voices got louder. The shiny path was real—the moon shone through my doorway.

I was lying in the shelter that Kamaka had built for me. It

was dark except for bright moonlight on the wall at my feet. I could see the crossed tree branches Kamaka had used to make the frame. I saw the tufts of grass he'd tied to the branches to keep my shelter dry. The voices were close—not on the rim of the Kauhakō volcano, but right outside the house.

I sat up and pushed my blanket aside, then crept to the doorway. Peering around the edge, I saw Kamaka's dark shape in the yard. The moonlight coming from out over the ocean probably made it easy to see him from the front. But the only thing I could see was his back—his large, dark shape. His head high, his shoulders wide, and his hands curling into fists and uncurling again.

Beyond him, just outside the stone enclosure, were more black shapes—men on horses, others on foot. A few of the men carried bamboo sticks stuffed with skewers of burning *kukui* nuts. In the half-light of the torches, I saw angry faces. From the center of the mob came Boki's voice.

"Kill the man! He has my woman. He has my boy. He stole my books."

Another voice joined Boki's. I recognized the voice of George, a constable who had been especially friendly with Boki. "Give them up, Kamaka. The woman you can keep, since she came with you. But return the books and the boy."

"Never!" declared Kamaka. "Nothing here belongs to that man. George, you should be ashamed of yourself. Your job is to protect the innocent, not to help the criminals."

The constable's voice responded from somewhere in the darkness. "It's hard to tell the good from the bad on Moloka'i," he said with a laugh.

"You've been drinking," said Kamaka. "Go home and sleep. Come back in the daylight when you're sober. Then we'll talk."

I heard more laughter, then Boki's voice. "Talk? Who wants

to talk?" Boki waved a long object in the air. "Don't reach for your gun," he said. "I have it. You were so busy healing the boy, you never noticed when it disappeared."

That was when I knew Kamaka was in real trouble. Boki had managed to steal his gun and convince the constable to cooperate with him. Kamaka was on his own against a drunken, armed mob. And it was my fault. If I had stayed with Boki, this would not be happening.

Boki and his crowd would not be reasoned with. I knew that. Boki would do everything in his power to lay his hands on whatever he wanted.

A figure pounced from the rock wall and knocked Kamaka to the ground. I heard Malia scream on the other side of my thatched wall, from inside her house.

Kamaka scrambled to his feet and tossed his attacker. But several more were in the enclosure now, wielding clubs. One of them moved in on Kamaka. While he was avoiding the first club, another one hit him on the shoulder.

"*Auē*!" I knew they would kill him if someone didn't do something. But who? Where was the *luna*?

That superintendent never could keep order in this place. Still, I would have to go after him. But then I realized they might kill Kamaka before I got back. I needed someone else to run with the message.

Ah Loy! Where was Ah Loy when there was really important news to carry?

I began to claw at the thatch on the back wall of my shelter. *Auē*! Kamaka had built it too well. But the sound of Boki's voice pushed me in my task.

"Kill him! I want him dead before the night is out. And I want that woman when you're done with him."

The scuffle outside continued. I tore at the thatch. And when

I had made a hole, I forced my head and shoulders through. I grasped at the rocky earth with my hand, pulling my body through the framework of my shelter.

"Pia!" a voice beside me whispered loudly.

"Ah Loy! What are you doing?"

"Watching the trouble. They are making much trouble for Kamaka!"

"Run, Ah Loy! Go for help! Get the *luna*!"

"But, Pia, the *luna* doesn't like to wake up in the middle of the night. He says that's what we have constables for."

I nearly shouted with frustration. "Go, Ah Loy! But first, stop at the home of Keona. She will know what to do."

I grabbed him by the shoulders and pulled him to his feet. He started to go but the fight pulled him back. He was torn between seeing the trouble for himself and being the first to tell someone else about it.

I gave him a shove. "Take Māui. He will get you there faster."

"Really? I can take your horse?" he asked. "I'll go quickly." Ah Loy ran to get Māui, who was hobbled at the edge of the enclosure.

I turned back to the trouble with Boki. I wanted to help. I *had* to help! But I could not stand against such a mob.

Malia's voice called loudly from the other side of the wall. "Lord, save us!"

I don't know when I joined her prayers. But *I* was helpless to save Kamaka, so I repeated the phrase with her, silently at first and then aloud. "Lord, save us!" And then I added, "And give Māui great speed!"

I sneaked around the side of my shelter. I peered around the front edge just as Kamaka staggered to the ground. I wanted to throw the bandits over the rock wall. To frighten them all away somehow. But there was nothing I could do to stop this crowd. Even if the *luna* arrived, his threats would not trouble them. I couldn't think of anything that would make them scatter.

Anything except ...

Except ... the Marchers of the Night! Every Hawaiian was afraid of them. Even those who claimed not to believe could be frightened by the ghost marchers.

I remembered a long-ago night on the mountaintop when Kamaka declared he was not afraid of the Night Marchers. *You would join them too, Pia,* he had said.

I thought fast. I hoped Hawai'i's gods would not punish me for what I was thinking to do. Noise, like the sound of drumming—that was what I needed. Chanting! I needed chanting. And torches.

I ran to the cooking area at the back of the hut. I reached for a gourd in the water bucket, huddled behind the hut, and began to tap out a rhythm. "Malia," I called through the walls of the house, "we need drums. Your *poi* calabash. Beat on the calabash."

Almost immediately I heard a steady rhythm. It was not as loud as a sharkskin drum, but it was all we had. Faster I played, and Malia played in time with me. But I needed more players. I needed chanters. Somehow I had to distract the mob out front.

"The Marchers of the Night!" I called. "They are coming. Move aside. Here come the Marchers of the Night."

I could not tell if anyone heard me. I could not stop drumming to look at the mob. I played loudly. I played steadily. And then, suddenly, I heard another voice rising above mine. It was a chanting. The high chant of Hawai'i's storytellers.

Had the Night Marchers really come? Suddenly I was terrified. I turned and saw the shadowy figure of Keona, standing just behind the enclosure. She leaned heavily on her crutch. But she held her head high. In a voice that was strong and full, she chanted one of her ancient Hawaiian stories. And it wasn't only Keona. Beside her stood Maka Nui, her head held high also, chanting with Keona. And somehow the chanting of those two sounded like all of Hawai'i had gathered in Kamaka's behalf. Behind them, in the distance, but coming closer, hoofbeats and torches rode the night.

I saw dark figures leaping out across the walled enclosure of Kamaka's home. The attackers were fleeing! I pounded harder on my gourd. I prayed in rhythm to my drumming. "Lord, save us! Lord, save us …"

Above the sounds of the calabash and the chanting, above the beating of horses' hooves, I heard the confusion out in front of the house. Horses neighed. Men screamed. Boki cursed.

A gunshot sounded.

Kamaka! Had Boki shot him? I had to know. I ran to the front of the enclosure. Kamaka lay in the dirt.

Then the *luna*'s voice rang out. "Go home, you filthy scoundrels, or you will be locked up before the night is out!"

"Yes," shouted Ah Loy, more boldly than the *luna* himself. "You will be locked up with no food for one week."

Boki laughed. "The *luna* has a little helper now. So he thinks he can put us in his jail." He looked around him and his voice trailed off as he realized he'd been deserted by those who'd come on foot.

Then I heard Keona's voice. "Shame on you, Boki!" She shook her crutch in Boki's direction. "I knew you before you learned to eat *poi* from your mother's finger. Your aging mother would die of heartache if she could see you now. Do I have to write and tell her what you've become? May God pour out His wrath on your shameful soul!"

At the mention of his mother, Boki grew quiet. I watched as

he slowly backed his horse away. I heard him call to the crowd, "Leave them alone for now. There will be other nights."

Boki turned his horse and headed toward the sea.

"Follow them!" shouted Ah Loy. He slapped Māui and led the way with a surprised *luna* following after.

I turned to Kamaka, lying motionless in the dirt. Malia cradled his head in her arms. Her tears ran down the side of his face and mixed with the blood that ran from his wounds. "Lord, save us," she pleaded. She repeated it again and again.

Blood leaked from the side of Kamaka's mouth.

I thought about the times I'd wanted to smash his face. Now, someone else had done it for me.

Why had I ever wanted such a thing?

Big, strong Kamaka was helpless. I reached past the shoulders of the crying women and put my hand on his chest. I felt it rise and fall in quick, shallow breaths.

He had survived. At least for now.

Malia grabbed my hand. "Do something, Pia. Please do something."

I knew that Kamaka's life was in my hands. And I wanted desperately to save him. I turned to Keona and Maka Nui. "Build a fire," I said. "Heat some water."

We needed breadfruit sap to stop the bleeding. But breadfruit trees do not produce in April. I considered the options. I didn't have time now to search for remedies in the forests beyond the peninsula. And besides, it would be dangerous to go looking. I had to use what was at hand.

I slipped off my shirt and began tearing it into strips. I handed Malia a rag to press against the blood coming from Kamaka's cheek. I tied a strip around a gash on his forehead.

When Maka Nui brought a pan of warm water, the women used my shirt to clean Kamaka's body. I probed and did not find any gunshot wounds. But I knew from his groaning that he had injuries I couldn't see.

Sometime during the night, clouds covered the moon, the wind began to blow, and it started to rain.

"We have to get him inside," I said.

Malia brought a woven mat to where Kamaka lay on the stony ground. Together we tugged at his broken body until he lay on the mat. Then we dragged him through the door of his house. Kamaka groaned and I felt hopeful that he would survive.

But it would take more than hope to keep him alive. And more than all my regrets. I would have to remember each healing plant Kamaka had shown me how to use. And return to Kamaka all the tenderness he'd ever given me.

26

Ka Mālama

[TO TAKE CARE OF]

In the days that followed, I searched for remedies in the wooded valleys to the east of the peninsula. I collected the salt residue from hollows by the sea and mixed it with the smashed pulp of *noni* fruit to make a poultice for Kamaka's cuts. I made a tea from *māmaki* leaves and instructed Malia to spoon it into Kamaka's mouth. "It will make him stronger," I promised.

Kamaka groaned as he slept. And on the second day, his body shook with a fever. He stared wide-eyed into the thatched ceiling and squirmed into a corner as if he saw someone up there threatening him. "No," he said. "Go away. I can't look at you."

I saw how this frightened Malia. "He's not talking to you," I said. "See, he's looking up there, at something else."

"I know," said Malia. "He sees someone we can't see." She stroked Kamaka's hair. "Shhh …" she said. "It's just us, Malia and Pia."

Kamaka whimpered like a young child. "Go away," he pleaded. "If I look at you I will get leprosy. Go away!" Malia jerked her fingers away from her husband's head.

I felt my own face. I fingered the lumps of leprosy and slowly backed away.

But Kamaka still cried, "I can't look at you."

I stood. "I have to get his fever down," I said. "Give him water on the spoon. I'll be back." I went out into the forest then, to collect *kī* leaves. As I rode Māui I kept thinking back to that long-ago night when I heard Kamaka dreaming on the mountain. He had said the same thing then—*I can't look at you.*

Who? Who couldn't he look at? Why did he have those dreams?

I filled a woven bag with *kī* leaves, and when I returned, I wrapped Kamaka's entire body with them. Malia gave him sips of cool water.

Dark shadows ringed Malia's eyes. Her hair was a tangle. She needed to sleep, but she stayed by Kamaka's side and did whatever I instructed.

Kamaka sweated and eventually the fever broke.

I leaned against the wall of the hut and closed my eyes. Sleep tugged at my eyelids, but Malia's voice interrupted. "Remember the day you told me why you hate Kamaka?" she asked.

I remembered. It was the day she'd caught me freeing Kamaka's pig. I sat with my eyes shut as though it would prevent Malia from seeing my shame.

But she wasn't thinking of my shame. She was thinking of her husband, and she was intent on telling his story.

"I asked him why he abandoned you when you got leprosy." Malia's words pulled me away from sleep. "Telling me was one of the hardest things he ever did. But he did tell me."

I sat in silence while Malia continued her story. She was so tired that her words came slowly, thickly.

"When Kamaka was young, only five years old, his mother sent him to the house of a neighbor for breadfruit. He walked alone on the path, and when he went around a curve a woman with leprosy was lying there. 'Help me,' she begged him. Her feet were rotten with gangrene. Kamaka breathed in that smell. Her tongue was swollen and her mouth would not close. Kamaka was so frightened he couldn't move. He stood, fastened to the ground, and screamed until his mother came."

Kamaka was five years old, I thought. *Before Kamaka knew me, he knew leprosy. Leprosy was his enemy before I became his friend.*

I tried to imagine Kamaka before I was there. To me, Kamaka had never been a child.

Malia continued her story. "His mother came when he screamed. She took him home to his *tūtū* and went back to help the woman. Later when she explained what had frightened him, his *tūtū* said an unfortunate thing. 'The foreigners say that leprosy is contagious,' she said. 'They act as if you can get it just by looking at it.'"

It was then that I understood what Kamaka had been dreaming about that night on the mountain. It wasn't the Night Marchers he didn't want to look at. It was leprosy.

Malia's eyes begged me to believe. "Pia, he was only a tiny child. He believed with his heart, not his mind. Nothing his family said could take away his fear. He dreamed about that woman. First he would smell her in his dreams and then she would grab him and beg him to look at her. He would wake himself with his crying."

I sat there in the small thatched house with only the tiny glow of a *kukui* nut lamp and looked at Kamaka's bruised body. Big as he was, Kamaka was really nothing more than a frightened child.

"I always thought he was so brave," I said.

"When I met him," said Malia, "he was the most desirable man I'd ever seen, the strongest, the bravest. But I liked him for some other quality I couldn't explain. He carried a sadness in him. It made me want to know him. Until I came here, I didn't learn that his sadness was for you. He moved to Kohala to get away from his shame, but it wouldn't let him go."

"And then you got leprosy," I said.

"Yes," said Malia. "At first when he knew it, he began having those dreams again. But after he came to Moloka'i, it was better. He still dreams, but not so much now. His fear—it's going away."

We sat in silence for a long time and I thought about Kamaka's fears. And mine, too. And Malia's. Finally I asked her, "What are *you* afraid of?"

Malia didn't take even a minute to think of her answer. "I'm afraid to see myself in the looking glass," she said. "My eyebrows. See?—they've fallen out."

She ran her fingers through her hair as if she suddenly felt embarrassed. She pulled a small comb from a wooden box and began to comb out the tangles in her hair, wincing in pain when she pulled at the knots.

"What about you, Pia?" she asked. "What are you afraid of?"

I breathed deeply. Then, because Malia had leprosy too, I began to say my fears. "The ones who die," I said. "Someone dumps them in a shallow grave. My mother won't even know when it happens. Will anyone sing or say prayers for me?"

I remembered the funeral of my aunt. I remembered the music—how it felt like a wave in the ocean. Like the curl of a perfect wave, the music had surrounded me. I had wept out my sadness while the singing carried me.

I sat in silence for a while, remembering, and then I said, "But I try not to think about dying. I think about other things. And I tell myself that it takes a long time for people with leprosy to die."

Malia crawled across the small room and sat beside me. She leaned her head on my shoulder. "Oh, Pia, what will become of us? Who will care when it's our time to die?"

"Shhh," I said. "Kamaka is getting well. He will care for you."

"And you, too, Pia. Kamaka will take care of *you,* too."

I knew it was true. Kamaka had cared for me once and he would do it again—if my leprosy didn't frighten him too much.

The oily *kukui* nuts in Malia's bowl burned low. I could barely see Kamaka's face in the darkness. But his deep breathing told me he was sleeping peacefully. No fever and no dreams of leprosy coming after him. It was time for all of us to get some rest.

But Malia was still talking. "Will they come back?" she asked. "Will Boki bring his men back to get us?"

"Not if Keona writes that letter," I said with a little laugh. "I think Keona discovered Boki's weakness. I wish we had known it a long time ago."

"But if he gets drunk again—or if he gives his liquor to enough people—it could happen." Malia shuddered.

I reached for a blanket that was rolled up in the corner. I wrapped it around Malia's shoulder. I pushed her gently until she lay on the mat beside Kamaka. I thought that Kamaka was lucky to have a woman who loved him so much.

"We need help, Pia," whispered Malia.

"Shhh. Don't tell me. Tell your God. Maybe He will do something about it."

"Maybe He will," said Malia. "Listen to this." She sat up and pulled a newspaper from the corner of her hut. I had already read the article she pointed to. It was about our leprosy settlement. But I listened anyway.

Malia held the newspaper close to the faint light. "'If a noble Christian priest, preacher or sister would be inspired to go and sacrifice a life to console these poor wretches, that would be a royal soul to shine forever on a throne reared by human love.'"

I agreed with the man who wrote the article. Some religious person *should* come to live here. But I didn't agree with Malia. I did not think God would send a missionary to sacrifice himself for us.

27

Makua Kamiano

[FATHER DAMIEN]

There was a day, the tenth of May in 1873, that stood out from all the others on Moloka'i. On that day, I awoke again to the sound of Ah Loy's voice. "Sail ho! It's Boat Day."

I opened my eyes. I looked past the grid of branches that formed the framework of my room, past the thick brown thatch of grass that kept out the wind and the rain. I looked through the door and into the late morning. It was a cloudy day and I felt the urge to go back to sleep.

But I couldn't do that. What if my mother had sent me a package? If something good came on the boat, I did not want to miss it. I jumped to my feet.

And anyway, Ah Loy was at my door. "Pia," he said, "I need Māui. I have to tell the people the boat is here."

"Take him," I said as I pulled on my trousers.

Ah Loy was convinced he had saved Kamaka's life by playing the constable. And ever since, he had thought of one excuse after another for riding Māui. I had learned not to mind. I had decided that Ah Loy deserved some pleasure in this place.

I heard nothing from Kamaka and Malia on the other side of the wall. They would probably sleep even later into the day. Kamaka was feeling almost well again, but he tired easily. He still had cuts and bruises but had gone back to working as a constable. The *luna* had even managed to get his gun for him.

I walked over to Keona's hut to see if Maka Nui wanted to come along.

"She certainly does," said Keona. "And I'm coming, too. Something extra good is coming on the boat today and I don't want to miss it."

I wondered how Keona knew what was on the boat. "I will wait for you," I said.

"No," said Keona, "you go ahead. Maka Nui is still waking up. I have to comb her hair. I'm sure one of my friends will come get me with their wheelbarrow."

I turned and hurried across the plain. I was glad Keona had her church friends to help her. Lately she seemed to be getting so feeble. She could barely walk anymore, and she slept much of the day.

Before I even got to the landing place, I could see Boki riding his horse through the crowd. Since his attack on Kamaka I'd managed to stay away from him, but I didn't know how I could avoid him now.

I found a place on the far side of the waiting villagers and looked around me constantly to be sure no one was sneaking up behind me.

The residents gathered as quickly as they could. Ah Loy rode Māui around to various people and supplied them with news. "Someone died last night," he said. "He's out there." Ah Loy pointed to a spot nearly in the center of the peninsula. "Who will bury him? Not me," he answered himself. "Not Boki for sure. Not Bad Albert."

Someday I could be found dead on the plain. Would Ah Loy go announcing my death to others who didn't care? Would anyone sing songs or pray for me?

"Whaleboat coming," said Ah Loy. He pointed through the mist. A long, dark shape lurched across the water. Inside, a band of people huddled against the wind. A man held on to his hat. A woman adjusted a flower tucked behind her ear. But the wind grabbed it and flew with it across the water—toward Oʻahu, away from the leprosy settlement.

Then I heard Kamaka's voice in my ear. "Pia, I'm going to help unload. If anything comes with your name on it, I will signal. Keep watch over Malia. She's sitting with Keona."

I nodded but did not look at Kamaka.

He pulled off his shirt and handed it to me for safekeeping. He waded into the waves, pushing through them until the water was up to his waist.

I smiled when I saw how strong Kamaka was. We weren't exactly friends, but helping Kamaka fight for his life had changed us. We had become partners in the struggle to survive, whether I wanted it or not.

But inside of me—that was different. Although I was relieved that he had lived, I kept a little place inside that did not let go of my anger.

The first person to get out of the whaleboat was an old woman, a large woman. I saw Kamaka wince as he and another constable shifted her heavy body onto the slippery rocks.

After the old woman came a girl about my age. She clung to Kamaka's strong shoulders. She did not cry or scream; she simply stared in quiet terror. I felt frightened for her. A beautiful girl like that would be an easy victim for someone like Boki or Bad Albert.

She staggered onto the rocks. She slipped and dropped her bundle when she caught herself. I lunged. I grabbed the bundle and then reached for the girl's hand to pull her up. It was bleeding.

"You cut yourself," I said. I looked into her dark eyes. "We will put salt and *noni* fruit on the wound."

Over the girl's shoulder, I saw Boki scowl. Someone cursed. It was Bad Albert—he wanted her! Albert reached into his pocket and pulled out a handkerchief. He shook the folds from it and held it out to her. "Let me wrap your wound for you," he said. "My house is nearby. I have ointments that work better than Hawai'i's remedies."

The girl looked at Albert and then at me. And back to Albert. He took her by the arm.

"Don't go with him!" I said, my voice loud and harsh. "He only wants to use you."

I grasped her other arm and pushed Albert away. Then I pushed the girl toward Keona. I saw a shadow then—Albert's shadow coming at me. I saw his clenched fists. I stepped aside and he missed me.

The force of his attack sent him to the ground.

Then I turned to face Boki. He held a walking stick, but he was not strong like Albert, and he did not attempt to hit me. I stood before him, legs apart and arms crossed.

"Have you forgotten our little visit?" asked Boki with a threat in his voice.

"I remember," I said. "I remember everything about you, Boki. And I am not afraid." I hoped Boki believed me more than I believed myself.

Behind me, I heard Keona's voice. "Boki, your mother will not be surprised to get a letter from me. But she may be surprised at what it says."

By now, Albert was on his feet again, cursing and pressing his handkerchief to a fresh scrape on his cheek. *Good,* I thought. *Go put ointment on your own wounds.* But I could see him glancing at me—and planning to come after me, too.

I'm sure it was Keona's threat that protected me, because Boki told Albert to leave me alone then. "And the girl, too," he said. "There'll be more where she came from." He pointed to the whaleboats coming from the steamer.

I backed away and let the two men scheme. I felt sorry for anyone they managed to prey upon. But I didn't know what to do about it. Protecting everyone in this place was more than even the constables could do.

I turned to watch Kamaka helping the new arrivals through the waves. I saw him squint to see who was coming toward him in the next whaleboat. Then I saw his mouth fall open and his eyes blink with surprise.

I turned to the boat that was coming to shore. In it were two men dressed in black like Catholic priests. It was not unusual for a priest to come occasionally to hear confessions and hold mass. But two priests at one time—that was unexpected!

Kamaka exchanged a quick *aloha* with the short, stocky priest in front, then took his bundle and handed it to another constable. The priest lifted the bottom of his robe so he wouldn't trip on it. Then he leaped from the small boat onto a large black rock. He wobbled for a moment but steadied himself and looked around. Something about him seemed familiar.

I saw that he wore spectacles with thick lenses. They slid down his nose when he jumped from the boat. So he stopped to adjust them. He pushed them into place. But still he squinted, as if to get a better look.

When he pushed at his spectacles I remembered the day that I first saw him. I was eight years old. Kamaka was fifteen. A sailing ship had arrived from Europe, so we rode our horses to Honolulu's harbor.

This priest had arrived with other missionaries on that ship. *And now he's coming here?* I thought. *To the leprosy peninsula?*

While I stood there wondering what this visit was about, Malia pushed past me.

Malia was not one to push and shove. Even when shipments had been delayed and we were all desperate for news from home, she would stand quietly and wait for the *luna* to find her mail. But now, suddenly she was tripping over her long dress to get to the front of the crowd.

What was she after?

I forgot to watch for Boki and Albert and even the beautiful girl I'd protected. I wanted to know what had changed Malia so. I followed her through the crowd. She elbowed her way to the front, pushing past old men and young women. But she stopped when one of the priests—the thin older man with the peaked face—raised his hand for silence.

The crowed hushed itself.

Malia stood still, but she was shaking. I was sure it was not the cold winds that had caused it. It reminded me of the way I had trembled on the day Kamaka came to Kalawao.

"I am Bishop Maigret," the thinner man said. "And this"— he put his hand on the shoulder of the stocky priest—"this is Father Damien."

Malia fell to her knees in front of the priest. "Kamiano!" she cried.

Father Damien knew her. "Malia, my child."

"Kamiano!" Malia was crying so hard that I could hardly understand her. "Have you come to live with us?"

The priest adjusted his spectacles as if to see all of us more clearly. I don't know what he expected to see. If he was Malia's priest, who had reached out to so many of our people, I was certain he'd already seen what leprosy could do. Surely he knew how it could mar a beautiful face or cripple a powerful body.

But I don't think he could have imagined just how frightening it would be to see so many of us in one place. Or to have such a crowd of us moving toward him with so much eagerness.

He staggered backward as though we'd actually pushed him. It was almost as if each one of us had touched him with our disease. He blinked a few times and looked to the *pali*.

And then, one by one, he looked into our eyes.

We waited to see what he would do with us. No one talked. The only sounds were Malia weeping and the roar of the constant ocean. The only movement was the wind whipping at our hair and clothing.

Finally, after he had examined each of us, Father Damien's eyes met mine.

"Yes," he said, as though I, and not Malia, had asked the question. "I have come to live with you."

28

Ka Manaʻolana
[HOPE]

I didn't believe that Father Damien would stay long in the leprosy settlement. His bundle was too small. I watched for a trunk or box with his name, but none followed.

He asked for a tour, so the *luna* led the way. Some of the residents walked, and a few, including Ah Loy, rode horses. Several people were pushed in wheelbarrows, and one or two rode on the backs of stronger neighbors.

I followed.

Malia walked beside the sturdy, energetic priest. "Kamiano," she said, "I prayed for mercy and you came."

"So many of my children have come here," said Father Damien. He kept looking around at us as if he was searching for someone he knew. "Have the others died? Where is Upa? Do you know Upa?"

Malia shook her head.

The question passed from one person to another. "Where is Upa?" Shrugs passed along, too. And shaking of heads. No one seemed to know this Upa. Not even Ah Loy.

"Maybe he's the man who died in the plain," said Ah Loy.

Piolani, the girl I'd protected, paid little attention to the priest. Instead, she watched everyone else.

And I watched *her.* Her face was round and her eyes were dark and lovely. But they showed her sadness. And why shouldn't they? She had lost her family when she came here.

Someone had covered her shoulders with flower garlands in every color. A circle of spicy leaves and red berries fit snugly on her head.

She did not walk with bowed head, as so many do when they first arrive. And she did not weep, either. But she blinked often as if she might be trying not to. She had a quietness about her, but I didn't think it was because she was new here. I thought she was probably always listening to others instead of needing them to pay attention to her.

Much later, after the bishop had left on the steamer, I stood in the doorway of Saint Philomena's, the Catholic chapel. Father Damien was there, unwrapping his bundle. He took out a book and placed it on the altar.

"See," I said. "He is here only to say quick prayers and hear confessions." I was just growling to myself, but Ah Loy, who sat on one of the straight wooden benches, heard me. He came and stood beside me in the doorway.

"Where will he sleep?" asked Ah Loy. His eyes followed the priest, who had picked up a palm frond and was sweeping the wooden floor of the small chapel.

"He has this church to sleep in," I said. "Probably even Boki won't bother him here."

"But Boki does not respect religion," said Ah Loy.

"No, he doesn't," I said. "But his mother thinks Father Damien is part of her 'ohana. Boki told me this. For her sake he will not bother the priest."

"And you were part of Boki's 'ohana too," said Ah Loy. "He was like a father to you."

"No!" I said. "Boki was not like a father." Surely Ah Loy could see this.

"So that is why you joined Kamaka's family?" said Ah Loy. "Kamaka makes a better father?"

Why was Ah Loy asking me these questions? What did he want with this information? Who did he want to tell it to?

I thought how Ah Loy had survived in this place—by carrying gossip from one part of the settlement to another. By delivering secrets that won him some trinket or a bit of food. On the day that Ah Loy and I arrived here, he had crowded into a house filled with boys and I headed for the valley to live by myself.

I ended up depending on Boki, but Ah Loy depended on no one. How had he managed it? And what was he trying to tell me now—that he wanted to be part of a family?

Or was he mocking me with these questions?

Suddenly I was angry. "Am I a child that I need a father to care for me? I am a man now." I poked his chest with my finger. "And *you*, Ah Loy, are a busybody!"

Ah Loy was surprised by my outburst. He stepped away from me, throwing his hands in the air and saying, "Sure, you are a man. Not a child, but a man." As he backed up, he nearly bumped into Father Damien, who had stopped sweeping to listen.

"Oh," said Ah Loy. "I beg your pardon, Father. I did not mean to walk in your path."

Father Damien nodded. He looked from Ah Loy to me. "What can I do for you?"

Was the priest mocking me? Did he think I needed him?

I did not intend to ask anything of this priest.

But Ah Loy—he was different. Ah Loy had something the Father could do for him. "Do you have a shovel?" he asked.

Father Damien stared blankly for a moment and then smiled. He held the palm frond out to Ah Loy. "No shovel," he said. "Only a broom. Do you want to borrow it?"

"There's a dead man out there," said Ah Loy, pointing toward the plain. "Who will bury him?"

Damien seemed confused by the question. "Whose job is it?" he asked.

Ah Loy explained that in Kalawao people didn't get a proper burial, especially if they didn't have friends.

"And that man," he said. "Even *I* don't know who he is."

Damien looked at the floor of the church that was only half-swept. He sighed and propped his leafy broom against a bench. "Who has a shovel?" he asked.

"Boki has a shovel," said Ah Loy.

"Boki?" I saw the priest's eyebrows go up. "Then get Boki's shovel," he said.

"Oh, no," said Ah Loy. "Boki is a very bad man." Then he turned and pointed toward me. "But Pia—he is not afraid."

Damien turned to me. "Get the shovel," he said quietly. "Together, we will bury the dead man."

I had not expected this priest to tell me what to do. "I cannot do that," I said. "Boki—"

But the priest interrupted. "Tell Boki the Father has need of it." Damien dismissed both Ah Loy and me, nearly pushing us out of his church with a wave of his hands. He followed us and closed the chapel door behind him. "Off with you, my children," he said. He laughed a little, as if he was trying to make a game of it. But I could see he expected me to obey him.

I walked slowly up the road toward Boki's house. I did not want to ask for the shovel, but Ah Loy had put me in this bad position. If I didn't do it, he would think little of me.

And the priest—what was it about him that made me do as he said?

This Father Damien could probably get whatever he wanted. I thought back to the day when I watched him arrive on the boat from Europe. I remembered how he had tried to convert Baldrik, the sailor. Even then, as young as I was, I could see that he was a man of determination. It was no use to argue with him.

Boki was playing cards on the *lānai* with Bad Albert and George, the constable. When he saw me, he snarled, "Why are *you* here? Are you already tired of that girl you stole from Albert at the landing?"

I did not look at Albert when Boki said this. But from the corner of my eye I saw that he touched the scrape on his cheek. I thought I should turn around and leave before he decided to throw *me* into the dirt. Surely one of Keona's friends had a shovel I could borrow instead.

But I had to show Ah Loy—and myself, too—that I was not a frightened child.

"I came for a shovel." I stopped and pointed to the plain. "There is a dead man," I said. "The priest wants to bury him."

Boki arched his one eyebrow in false surprise. "A dead man? On Moloka'i? How could it happen?" Then he interrupted his own poor humor with a cold stare. "Go away," he said.

I stood just inside the rock wall that surrounded Boki's yard. I could not stay there because Boki would not allow it. And I could not leave. Ah Loy was waiting for me to fail. I could not let that happen.

Boki was a weak man; his body had grown thin and his cough was relentless. I could run faster and hit harder than he could. But he was a man of means, and for that reason he was as powerful as ever. If Boki gave the command, George or Albert could throw me down in the road and trample me.

Ah Loy had followed me. He stood nearby, watching to see what would happen.

I pretended I was not frightened. "I need the shovel."

"Go away," Boki said.

I knew where the shovel was tucked under the floor of the

house, so I snatched it up and hurried away. But I heard footsteps—Boki had sent George after me.

"Stop!" George yelled. He raised his club and grabbed me by the arm. His grip was as mean as Boki himself. But I looked him full in the eye.

"The priest sent me," I said. Surely George would have some respect for religion, I thought. Perhaps that would save me.

"I can arrest you."

I wanted to tell George he was a poor excuse for a constable, but that would anger him. So I tried to keep my voice steady. "I am not a criminal."

"Stealing is a crime."

"Borrowing is not. It is the priest who borrows it. Will you arrest a priest?"

Now I saw that Boki had followed us. He leaned heavily on his walking stick and his breathing came hard.

"Look," I said. "Soon it will be you, Boki. Maybe if you act like a Christian, the Father will bury *you* when your time comes."

Boki's eyes narrowed. Maybe he was thinking of his mother, who no longer had her priest. Or maybe he was thinking that the priest could send her a bad report if he behaved poorly.

"Father Damien will escape from this place long before I need a burial," he growled. "But go take the shovel to him. If he sees what he's gotten himself into, he'll leave even sooner."

I knew then that my words had found Boki's weakness. He could feel his death coming as surely as I could see it.

Boki turned and headed back to his house, and I carried the shovel to Father Damien. He was standing in the middle of the road near one of Kalawao's homes. The woman who lived there leaned across her gate to talk to him. "We begged the bishop to send us a Father," she said. "But we never believed it would happen."

The priest smiled. "We cannot predict the ways of God." Then he turned and walked with Ah Loy and me toward the center of the peninsula.

I knew when we were nearly there. I knew because the smell of death rode on the wind. I gagged, and I heard Father Damien gasp. He stopped suddenly, and his chest heaved beneath his black robe.

Ah Loy pinched his nose. "There he is," he said.

I saw Father Damien's face change. It had been so strong when he ordered me to get the shovel. Now everything about it drooped and trembled.

He moved cautiously past Ah Loy, peering to where the body lay in the weeds. Then he jerked his head away and staggered backward. He turned his back on the body in the grass and for a long time he stared out to sea.

Was he searching for the steamer? Did he regret letting the boat leave without him?

The smell of this death was all over us now. I wanted to turn and run. But I had learned on my first day here that I could never really escape.

Ah Loy came to where I waited with the shovel resting in the earth. "I think it is his Upa," he whispered.

We stood with our shirts pulled over our noses and watched the priest. The wind tossed his thick brown hair and billowed the skirt of his black robe. Slow tears traveled down his tanned cheeks. He lowered his head and his body shuddered. His tears fell into the grass.

"See how much he loved him," said Ah Loy.

I didn't know if it was Upa. But it didn't matter who the dead person was. Suddenly I felt that it was all of us—Ah Loy, Keona, Maka Nui, and Malia. And me, too.

This death was our death. And this priest was weeping for us.

After a long time, Father Damien turned to me. "Give me the shovel," he said. He sounded angry.

Father Damien walked back to the body and began to dig nearby. A cloud of dust rose and settled on his clean black robe. I saw that his robe hid powerful muscles. He worked quickly and growled at the rocks whenever his shovel rang against them.

"Lots of rocks on Moloka'i," said Ah Loy.

The priest gave him a sharp glance and went back to his digging. He dug for a while, and then he stopped and walked away for clean air. He came back and worked some more. His chest heaved and he turned away often to breathe. Sometimes I thought he was ready to quit. But he did not.

Finally he stopped and looked at me and then at Ah Loy. "Who is going to help me?" he asked.

Ah Loy backed up, then stopped. He stayed close enough to see everything but too far away to help.

I turned and walked toward the sea. But I didn't see the ocean's deep blue color. Even with my back to the wooded valley I saw a pig snuffling in a ditch. I felt the terror of that first day.

I didn't want to look at the body beside the priest. Seeing it would be harder than asking Boki for his shovel. Helping to bury it would be worse than getting hit with George's club.

But what if it were *my* body decaying in the dirt?

I thought how I had bullied Boki into lending the shovel. I would die just as surely as he would. I came to this place knowing it. And every day I saw it again.

I took a deep breath and went to where the priest waited. I did not look at the body. I simply picked up stones and hurled them behind me. And I stopped often to run away for clean air.

The priest did, too.

What kind of man is this, I wondered as I watched him work. *Why did he come here? Isn't he afraid of death?*

After a while, I took my turn with the shovel.

When the job was finished, Ah Loy spoke. "Was it Upa?" he asked.

The priest didn't answer at first. But then he shook his head. "I couldn't tell."

I supposed we would never know who Upa was. He could have come here without any of us knowing and died without anyone caring.

At least until the priest arrived.

I had thought that when Father Damien prayed, his voice would be loud so that God could hear him in His heaven. Instead, it was just above a whisper.

We walked back to Kalawao with the priest leading the way. Even Ah Loy was silent. I thought about Father Damien's prayer, and I wondered if God had always been on this peninsula, listening to our feeble voices.

It was dark when I returned the shovel. I slipped quietly around Boki's house and slid it beneath his floor. Then I walked back toward the church. Ah Loy was there, perched on a rock wall, watching.

"He is going to sleep under the *hala*," Ah Loy reported. He pointed to the small tree beside the church. "Lots of bugs to be his friends."

I thought of the scorpions that could share the priest's bed. And the dampness that would chill him, and the stones that would dig into his flesh.

Why wasn't he sleeping inside the church? Did Catholics have rules about that? Surely God wouldn't mind if a priest took shelter in His house, would He? Or was there some other reason why Father Damien slept on the ground like a poor outcast?

This day had brought so many questions.

I turned and slowly crossed the plain. When I neared

Kamaka's house, I saw the glow of a fire and the dark shapes of people gathered around it. I recognized the snuggled shape of Kamaka and Malia as well as Keona and Maka Nui. But there was someone else there, too.

It was Piolani.

I stopped for a moment and watched. I listened to the crickets in the grass, the waves crashing out on the shore, and the low whistle of the wind. And then I heard another sound.

"Amazing grace, how sweet the sound that saved a wretch like me ..." I had not heard such a clear, sweet song since coming to this place.

I saw that it was Piolani who sang. Firelight played across her face. The breeze lifted her hair.

And it seemed to carry with it a gentle *aloha*.

29

Ka Make

[DEATH]

The new priest slept under the *hala* tree each night until a boat delivered lumber for him to build a house. I went to the landing place to watch the ship unload his boards. Father Damien started calling out orders as soon as the lumber was unloaded. He knew many of us by name already.

"Pia," he called, "carry these boards to the oxcart." Then he called for someone else to give him a hand. When we had them all loaded and the oxen had pulled them across the peninsula, he began to measure and cut. I helped hold the boards steady while he pulled his saw back and forth, back and forth. Sometimes his hand touched mine, but he did not pull away or seem afraid of leprosy.

Ah Loy and the others wanted to take a turn, so I let them. I sat on the ground and watched the priest making work into a game with his group of boys. The little children watched, too. Wherever the Father was—that was where the children of Kalawao wanted to be.

But they couldn't follow him everywhere.

There were many interruptions to his project. The people were learning quickly that the priest would come at a moment's notice if someone was dying. "Off I am," he would say, and the building of his house would have to wait.

One more night for him under the *hala* tree.

Every morning Damien met with the Catholic believers in

their church building. Malia always attended. I did not, but I knew he was gaining converts. Malia and Ah Loy reported regularly about some new person he was baptizing.

At first I was unsure of myself around the priest. He was so demanding, and he liked to have things go his way. But no one could call Father Damien selfish. We saw that he wanted good things for his "little children." That was what he called us, the people of the settlement. To him, even Kamaka and Boki were his children.

And he *was* like a father to all of us.

Soon after he arrived, the Board of Health opened a store so that we could buy clothing, tools, and household items. And the board began to issue checks for each one of us. It was only six dollars a year, but at least we could choose a little something for ourselves.

I was in the store one day looking at a case with knives and thinking about whether I should buy one or spend my money on clothing.

Father Damien was there, too, talking happily to the storekeeper until he realized he'd lost the checks he was holding for some of the patients. "Wait a minute," he said. "I had them right here. I know I had them. Where could they be?"

He asked everyone in the store if we had seen them. I don't know if someone else had, but I hadn't. And everyone told him they hadn't either.

By this time, Father Damien knew about the crime that went on in this place. "Who could have taken them?" he asked.

One of the children grabbed the priest's hand and pointed to me. "Pia is a thief," he said.

The priest came to me then and gripped my shoulders. "Have you seen those checks?" he asked. His eyes were filled with tears.

"No," I said. I was ashamed for the Father to know that I had been one of the criminals in this place. "Please believe me. I do not steal anymore."

Ah Loy came to my defense then. "Pia speaks true," he said. "He is not Touch Hands now."

After Father Damien turned away, he saw some paper lying on the floor. He grabbed it, hoping that it was one of the checks, but it was not. He searched in every corner of the store. "What will my poor children do without their allowance?" He rushed out the door and went to see the *luna*.

That's how Father Damien was. He cared about every single one of us, and he knew we needed much more than our six dollars would buy.

Usually we depended on our families to send us extra money if they could. But one day Kamaka told me how we could earn some. "Pita Kaeo needs some men to clear the rocks from around his house," he said. "I promised to find help. Do you want to come?"

Part of me did not want to cooperate with Kamaka. But another part of me wanted to work side by side with him as if nothing had ever gone bad between us. Sometimes it felt impossible to live so close to him and still keep my distance.

I followed him to Pita Kaeo's house. Pita was a member of Hawai'i's royal family. He had arrived in the leprosy settlement only a few months after Father Damien came.

The royal cousin was a fleshy man with sleepy eyes. I could see him through the window of his house. He sat there reading but could not seem to pay attention to his book. He came often to the door to watch us work. After we had filled an oxcart with rocks, Pita called to Kamaka, "Come here."

Kamaka leaned his pickaxe against the stone pile and walked over to Pita's porch. I couldn't hear what Pita said, but I saw him lead Kamaka to different places around his yard. Giving orders came easily to him. I could see it in the way he used both hands to point this way and then another.

Kamaka came back and reported on their conversation. "After we haul the stones away, he wants to plant mangos and other trees here. He says his cousin Queen Emma will send more trees as soon as we dig the holes."

I stared at the little house with Pita standing in the doorway dreaming of trees he would grow nearby. I thought about the fruit that those trees would provide, and the seeds that would become more trees.

"Finally," I said. "It is about time for someone to plant trees in this place." I turned and looked around me. I imagined trees—mango, papaya, and banana—spreading across the peninsula. But that would take a long time. And I would likely never see it.

While I stood there and looked across the grassy plain, I saw a child running toward me. It was Maka Nui.

"Pia! Come, Pia! Hurry!"

I ran to Maka Nui and saw that she was crying. I knelt in the dirt beside her. "What is the matter?" I asked.

She wept into my shoulder.

"What?" I demanded, shaking her gently.

"Tūtū is dead," sobbed Maka Nui.

Keona? Dead? She can't be! I sank to the ground and pulled Maka Nui onto my lap. "Are you sure?" I demanded.

"Yes," cried Maka Nui. "I went with Piolani to the store. When we came back, Tūtū was lying with her face in the dirt."

Kamaka nudged my shoulder. "Go with her," he said. "I'll tell Pita we need to leave."

I held tightly to Maka Nui as we crossed the plain to Keona's hut. Before we got there, Kamaka caught up to us. He picked

Maka Nui up in his strong arms and carried her. I followed, wondering what it would feel like to be carried again—to lean on Kamaka when I felt weak.

As we climbed over the last stone wall before Keona's house, I saw Piolani huddled over the old woman's body. I heard her sobbing as I approached. And no wonder—Keona had become her *tūtū* as soon as she arrived in Kalawao. And in the months that followed, they had truly become *'ohana*.

I looked at Piolani and her weeping reminded me of Malia, crying in the whaleboat when she arrived at Moloka'i. I remembered how Kamaka put his arms around her and how she wept onto his chest.

I wanted to comfort Piolani as Kamaka had comforted Malia.

I put one arm around Maka Nui. With my other hand I touched Piolani's shoulder. The wind lifted her long black hair and brushed it across my arm.

Piolani leaned against my leg. "She was my family," she sobbed.

"We'll take care of you," I said. "You can live with us and be part of our *'ohana*. We are all family already."

"Yes," said Kamaka in a voice that was low and husky, "we are all family already."

Later, after Malia arrived, she and Piolani washed Keona's body. I helped Kamaka place her on a blanket, and we carried her between our shoulders. We took her to Father Damien's small house beside the church. But Damien was not home.

"Where is the priest?" we asked a man who was walking on the road. The man turned and pointed to the low building that Kalawao called its hospital. I ran to the hospital but stopped at the door. I did not want to see Kalawao's dying patients.

"Father Damien?" I called.

"I'm here." The voice came from across the room. "Come in, Pia."

I peered inside. I saw that the patients no longer lay on the floor. They had real beds now. But it still smelled foul. I wished the priest would come to the door. But he was busy. He would not come until he was ready.

"What is it?" asked Damien. "Is there a problem?"

"Keona is dead." I did not hear the Father's response because a patient called out for water just then. I took one last breath of clean morning air and dashed to the priest's side.

He was rubbing salve into blackened wounds. I gagged and turned to go.

"Wait," said Father Damien. "*Who* died?"

"Keona."

The priest paused in his task and gazed out the window. He was smoking his pipe, and I caught the scent of it. The powerful smell of tobacco covered the smells of rotting flesh and filthy blankets. So that was why he smoked a pipe!

Father Damien removed the pipe and held it there in his hand. "I am sorry for your sake." He looked as if he wanted to cry, too. "And I am sorry I was not there when she died."

I knew that Father Damien had tried to convert Keona to his Catholic faith. He was probably worried that he had not been there to save her soul at the last minute. But I was sure that Keona had gone to a good reward.

She had been the first person I saw when I arrived at the landing place. I could still see her quarreling Maka Nui right out of Bad Albert's arms. I felt weak just thinking about how bad life would have been for Maka Nui if Albert had taken her in.

And for Piolani, too.

I turned and walked slowly to the bright doorway. I stepped out into the August morning and leaned against the hospital wall.

Even when I trusted no one else, I had loved Keona. Even when I thought anger was all I needed to survive, I had counted on her wisdom. What would Kalawao be like without her?

In a few minutes, Father Damien came outside. "We have a coffin ready," he said. "Ah Loy has been helping us build them."

He led me to the storage building beside his house.

We lifted Keona into a box. Malia placed a bright *lei* of orange berries around Tūtū's neck, and Maka Nui kissed both her cheeks and rubbed noses with her.

Keona's friends dug a grave by the Church of the Healing Spring.

Father Damien went into his house, and when he came out he was wearing a different robe. The one he worked in was nearly always spattered with mud or sawdust. But this robe was clean.

In some ways Father Damien was like a different person in that clean robe. His hair was freshly combed and his hands were washed. He did not dash about from one task to another. Now he moved more slowly and he spoke quietly.

"Keona has made an example for us," he said. "Let each of us strive to live as she did."

We took her to the Church of the Healing Spring. Kalawao's wind chilled us even though the sun was shining. I huddled with Keona's church friends in a circle of comfort. Some of them recited scripture and sang hymns. Then we put the coffin in the ground. While we covered it over with dirt, Piolani sang. Her voice broke, but she would not stop until the song was finished.

As we stood there by Keona's grave, with the sound of the ocean behind us, Father Damien told us he wanted to form funeral societies. "I need help to prepare the bodies and give our people a proper burial," he said.

Malia stepped forward. She fingered the prayer beads she wore around her neck. "I will help," she promised the priest.

"Bless you, my child," said Father Damien. Then he put his hand on Piolani's shoulder. "Your music is a gift to our people. We will start a choir. Then we'll always have music for funerals. Will you help me?"

Piolani nodded. The tears in her dark eyes spilled over now that she had finished singing. But she smiled at the same time, and I could see that she was pleased to have a gift for Kalawao.

30

Ka Huikala

[TO CLEANSE]

I suppose the sun did not shine more after Father Damien arrived, but sometimes it seemed that way. The days felt warmer. And the peninsula looked less brown.

I often rode Māui through the settlement just to catch a glimpse of Father Damien at work.

One day more than a year after the priest arrived, I was down by the water trying to catch some shrimps. The water was calmer than usual and did not feel so dangerous. It made me want to swim far out into the ocean. Maybe toward Oʻahu. I knew it was impossible. But still, sometimes I wanted to try.

Even if they caught me and sent me back here, maybe I could see my family for a few minutes. Perhaps it would be long enough to see how my sister had grown. And to place my mother's face in my mind again.

I never told my mother why I no longer lived with Boki. I simply told her that I had moved to Kamaka's house. Even if I couldn't remember her face, it made me feel good to think how that would make her smile. She didn't need to know that Kamaka and I weren't really *ʻohana* in the way we once had been.

While I stood at the water's edge and thought about these things, I heard footsteps behind me. I turned to see Ah Loy.

"Did you hear?" Ah Loy asked. "Boki is dead. Father Damien sent me to get you."

Boki dead? It should have made me glad. But I did not feel joy.

I turned toward Boki's house. I could not see it from where I stood. I was down on the rough beach below the piles of black rocks that edged the peninsula. But I remembered the first time I saw it. I was standing on top of those lava rocks, cold and wet, lost on the black edge of a tiny peninsula. I heard again Boki's voice offering shelter. I saw his one good eye. And I did not trust it.

Not then, anyway.

I remembered the hunger and sickness that drove me into Boki's house. And the relief of sleeping there. I remembered the warm blankets and good clothing he provided.

Maybe he had saved my life. I thought about haircuts and sweet potatoes. I thought about Keona threatening to tell Boki's mother how bad he'd become. I remembered my yellow cat. And Kamaka bleeding in the dirt.

"Why did Father Damien send for me?" I asked. But I had a feeling I knew already.

Ah Loy shrugged.

"Don't you know everything that happens here?"

Ah Loy threw up his hands. "But I don't know about that priest," he said. "He is full of surprises. Remember when we had to walk to the stream for our water? Now look—we have it in our village. Why? Because the government sent pipes and Damien helped us get water. And at Christmas we had a celebration. We were miserable here, but Father Damien is making us happy."

Ah Loy was anxious to go to the Father. "Hurry!" he said. He climbed onto Māui, who waited for me not far from the sea. So I climbed on behind Ah Loy and let him guide us to the large field near Father Damien's church.

The priest was playing there with a noisy band of children when we arrived. I watched him run and shout and fall playfully into the dirt. They were playing tag-me-not.

But, of course, Father Damien let the children tag him.

He had never been afraid to touch any of us with leprosy. The visiting doctors eyed us from a safe distance and left bottles of ointment for the *luna* to distribute. But Damien rubbed the salve into our wounds.

Always I wondered, *Why isn't he afraid of us?*

"Pia," boomed Damien's big voice. He gently shook off the playful children. "Go now," he told the little ones with a kind firmness. "You have played me too hard already. Pia, you are here. Come." He beckoned to me with a jerk of his head and strode away so fast that his long robe made a snapping sound with each step.

I climbed down from my horse. I had learned on that first day that when this priest gave an order he expected others to obey. I started slowly up the road.

"I'm coming, too," said Ah Loy.

"Of course you are," I said.

I followed Father Damien to his house. He handed me a shovel. "We need to dig a grave."

I stared at the shovel. "Boki?"

Damien nodded.

"No! I won't do it."

"I was with him before he died," said the priest. "He confessed his sins and God forgave him."

I gripped the shovel so hard I saw my brown knuckles go white. *God can forgive Boki if He wants to*, I thought. *But that doesn't mean I'm going to.*

"Come," said Damien. He took off at a pace that set his robe flapping.

"Go!" said Ah Loy.

I had no intention of digging a grave for Boki, but I hadn't learned to say no to this priest. So I followed him to the graveyard beside his church. Damien took the shovel from my hand and began to dig. He talked as he worked. "I'll be enlarging the church," he said. "It's too full for our growing flock of believers."

With the tip of his shovel, he worked a rock out of the soil. He motioned for me to move it. I picked up the rock and tossed it behind me. Damien uncovered another stone, and I moved it out of his way, too.

"And I'll have to enlarge the graveyard," said Damien. "It's overflowing."

I heard the sadness in the priest's voice and wondered how he could care about Boki. The priest was a tough man who didn't tolerate wickedness. But when it came to forgiveness, he was like a child.

When *I* was a child, it didn't matter what Kamaka did to make me angry—I could never be upset with him for long. But that was before leprosy. Before I lost him. And my family, too.

I looked at Father Damien, and for the first time I thought about *his* family. It must have been a long time since he had seen them—it was now nearly ten years since that day when I first saw him get off the ship in Honolulu. That was before the government had even created this leprosy prison.

Why had he come to Hawai'i? And especially to Moloka'i?

"Did that bishop send you here?" I asked him.

The Father stopped digging and looked at me then. "The bishop asked several of us to take turns," he said. "And so I volunteered."

"Oh." I wondered if that meant he would be leaving after all. "When will it be someone else's turn?" I asked. "Will you go back to Kohala?"

Father Damien shook his head. "I cannot leave my children in these conditions."

"But you don't have leprosy. What if you *never* get to leave?"

Damien turned away from me then, and I saw his eyes moving about, looking over the scattered cottages of Kalawao. "If I never leave this place," he said softly, "I will be the happiest missionary in the world."

Happy? In Kalawao? Never seeing his family again? Never traveling to Honolulu or Kohala? How could anyone love God that much? How could anyone love *me* that much?

I just didn't understand.

"Pardon me for the questions, Father, but, but ... do you plan to die here?"

Damien looked up to the *pali* then, and I could see that he was remembering something. "I died before I came," he said. "When I took my religious vows, I prostrated myself before the altar and my brothers placed a funeral shroud over me. On that day I died to my own will. God's will became my will."

He raised his arm and moved it in a wide path in front of him that included all of Kalawao. "This is God's will for me. Pia, *you* are God's will for me."

The Father was so intent on making me understand that he did not remember to dig Boki's grave. He just stood with his hand on the shovel and looked into my eyes. Was he saying that God wanted him to come to us? That God knew how desperate we were for Him to live among us?

Then Father went back to wrestling with the rocky soil. His soft grunts kept time to the rhythm of his shovel. I stared at his calloused hands that had dug so many graves in Kalawao, even for criminals.

And I knew *I* would not be left in a ditch to rot. As I realized this, I also knew I could not let Father Damien dig Boki's grave alone.

"Let me dig," I said. I reached for the shovel.

Damien handed it to me. "I'll toss the stones aside for you," he said.

I put the tip of the shovel under the edge of a stone. I wiggled and shoved and heaved until I lifted it out of the dirt. Damien tossed it behind us. I pushed the shovel into the ground again and jumped with my bare feet on top of the blade. I put all my weight and a great deal of my anger into that jump.

"*Auē!*" said Father Damien. "Don't do that!"

I looked at the priest in surprise. "What did I do?"

"Your feet. You must take better care of them. Let me look." Damien pushed me gently into the pile of dirt that would soon cover Boki's body. He took one of my feet in his hands and probed the bottom of it with his fingernail. "Can you feel that?"

I shook my head.

"Since you don't feel pain, you must be extra careful. See? It's bleeding. You broke these sores." He shook his head and examined my other foot. "This is not good," he said. "Come with me. Ah Loy will dig while I tend to your feet."

Ah Loy was lying on the ground, soaking up the laziness of the day. "B-but," he sputtered. "I, I, you ..."

Father Damien waved him off. "Just a little more digging," he said.

He put his hand on my shoulder and walked me to his little house beside the chapel. "Come inside," he told me. He slid a wooden chair over to a window, and I sat down. I looked around his house. He didn't have much—a chair, a table, a map of the world on the wall. A small pile of dishes that needed washing. And a wooden bowl with fresh eggs.

I could hear his flock of chickens clucking outside his window. It was a comforting sound. A sound from home. I had seen the chickens pecking the earth around Damien's feet, enjoying his attentions. And I'd seen him giving eggs to the people of Kalawao.

Damien poured clean water into a basin and lifted my foot inside. I could not feel the coolness of the water on the bottom of my foot. But I felt a warmth spreading throughout the rest of me as the priest gently lathered my foot with soap and water. He lifted my other foot into the basin, and I felt as though the Father was washing more than my feet—that somehow even the wounds inside me were being cleansed by his touch.

"If you let this go, it will get much worse," he said. "This is why so many of the patients have lost their feet and hands. They don't feel pain, so they don't protect themselves from dangerous wounds. That's why their sores become infected."

The priest reached for a jar of salve on the windowsill. He rubbed the ointment into my wounds. Then he found a clean cloth, tore it into strips, and wrapped them around my feet. "Even if you won't wear shoes," he said, "you *must* protect your feet."

I knew the Father was right—I should be wearing shoes. But I did not like them, so I had been careless.

Father adjusted his spectacles. He looked full in my eyes and I saw that his lenses were spattered and dusty. *How can he even see through them?* I wondered. But I had the feeling that the priest could see through the dirt into that hard, angry place inside me.

"You must not let the numbness destroy you," he said. "It would be better if you could feel the pain."

He did not mention the numbness I had kept around my heart. He did not tell me that my unfeeling spirit would destroy me as surely as the numbness in my feet could. But I did not need a priest to tell me that. I had lived long enough in Kalawao to see that anger only led to misery.

And I had seen what a Father's love could do in this place.

31

Ka Ho'oponopono

[TO PUT THINGS RIGHT]

I went to Boki's funeral. During the service, Father Damien talked about the damage Boki had done. "He hated me, too," he said. "When I broke up his drunken parties, Boki found ways to get revenge. But if our Savior can forgive the men who tortured and killed Him, can I do any less?"

He paused and looked at each of us one by one. "Revenge is not my task," he said. "My task is to forgive."

A small choir of patients sang for Boki, as they did now for every person who died here. Many of the voices were diseased and raspy. But Piolani's voice rang clear. I felt her melody picking me up, moving me from a dark, damp place to a sunlit plain.

I thought about the things the Father had told me while we dug the grave. How he lay under the funeral cloth and chose death. How he came *here* to die.

How he was happy here.

I needed to get outside, where I could think about this. I hurried out of the chapel and sat on a stone wall near the graveyard.

So many things had changed with Damien's arrival. I knew that I was slowly dying, but Kalawao had begun to feel like a place for living.

I also knew that, as much as I tried, I couldn't really live without Kamaka. After all, hadn't he been there from the beginning?

I thought again about my childhood in Honolulu. I could see in my mind the way Kamaka raced across the sand on Pele so fast that his hat would blow off and he'd have to circle back to pick it up. I remembered his stories of sightseers and Night Marchers. I saw him diving with arms outstretched into a deep pool of water. And I heard his laughter.

Like Father Damien, Kamaka had come here knowing it was a place to die. Kamaka was not a priest who chose death for the sake of God. But he did not have leprosy, either.

Why had he come? For Malia only?

Was it possible that what Malia had told me was true? Had Kamaka come to make right his wrongs? Could he have come here for me?

I knew that I could never return to those days in Honolulu. But Kamaka was here on Moloka'i, and I *could* go back to being his friend.

I sat for a long time and thought about whether I could forgive.

I don't know exactly when I chose it. I know only that I untied my horse from the fence in front of Father Damien's whitewashed house. I climbed on Māui and rode across the plain.

I expected Kamaka to be planting mango trees at Pita Kaeo's house, but before I got there I saw him riding toward me on Pele.

When we met on the trail, I did not urge Māui to pass. I did not avoid looking into Kamaka's eyes.

His deep brown eyes searched mine.

I wanted to tell him that I no longer hated him. But I didn't know how to say it. Finally I turned Māui around so that we both faced Kalawao and the sea. I pointed past the leprosy village to the little island that poked itself out of the water.

"See Ōkala?" I asked. "Let's swim out there and climb to

the top. We could plait palm leaves together and hang on to them while we jump. It would be like flying."

Kamaka looked to Ōkala and then back to me. His eyes grew wide and then crinkled nearly shut as a slow smile spread across his fine brown face. His nose twitched and his smile grew into a laugh. He gave a joyful hoot. "Okay!" He slapped his horse into a run.

I did not follow him.

I wanted to. I wanted to climb onto Pele and hang on to Kamaka and ride to the sea. But I sat there instead. Sat on Māui and admired the look of Kamaka, the way he threw his head and shoulders back. I could tell even with his back to me that he was laughing. His happiness made me want to follow.

But still I sat and watched.

Before Pele had gone very far, Kamaka slowed her down, circled around, and came back to ride beside me.

We rode slowly across the peninsula, and I saw it differently now—the sunny place back on the western side where Kalaupapa village was, the tired volcano in the center, and the brown plain before us. I saw the whitewashed shacks, and the hospital of Kalawao. I looked at the Protestant church that Keona had loved and the Catholic one with our beloved Father there holding a funeral. A hymn spilled out its windows.

Now I knew for sure that God had joined us here. I knew because His *aloha* was changing us.

Was changing me.

I was a lost child who had found his way home. A *kalo* corm attached to a healthy plant. I was the old Pia—connected to the old Kamaka.

And yet both of us were new.

We left our horses at the top of the ledge that bordered the sea. We scrambled down its side and stripped off our shirts.

This was the spot where the whaleboat had brought me ashore. A place where stormy waters often made it dangerous for swimming.

But on this day it was calmer than usual—just right for playing.

So I pushed Kamaka into the water, and of course he pulled me in, too. Above the roar of the waves I heard his laughter. But he did not hold me under the water to prove how strong he was. And he did not begin swimming to Ōkala, either.

Instead he waited for me to lead.

I looked into his dark eyes, and when I did, I saw a man who did not have to be the first or the strongest. He had already admitted that he was sometimes weak. He did not need to appear fearless, because his fear had been exposed.

And yet, in spite of his weakness, it seemed to me that Kamaka was stronger than ever.

I dived into the water and swam toward Ōkala. And I felt, as I swam, that I was becoming stronger, too. That even if these waters had been stormy on this day, they could not have kept me from swimming with Kamaka.

AUTHOR'S NOTE

For centuries people believed that leprosy was highly contagious. Responses to the disease differed from place to place, but societies around the world protected themselves by casting people with leprosy out of their villages. In Europe, during the Middle Ages, those suffering from leprosy were forced to attend their own funerals, at which black cloths were lowered over them. Then they were banished from their towns and villages.

Leprosy probably came to Hawai'i in the early 1800s. The people of Hawai'i had embraced visitors and new residents from many countries. Tucked away in some foreigners' bodies were the germs of deadly diseases that Hawaiians could not fight off—venereal diseases (now called sexually transmitted infections), smallpox, and others, including leprosy.

Leprosy was frightening mostly because it brought disabilities and changed a person's physical appearance. This created a social stigma, at least with the many non-Hawaiian people who lived in the islands. It also caused nerve damage that prevented patients from feeling pain. As a result, the patient might injure himself without even feeling it. Infections would set in. Neglect and unsanitary conditions contributed to the decay of flesh and other problems. People did not die from leprosy itself but rather from complications related to the disease.

Such were the conditions Pia found when he arrived in Kalawao.

THE KALAWAO SETTLEMENT
The Board of Health had not expected life to be so difficult in the Kalawao settlement. Government officials had purchased a tract of land that would isolate the patients from the rest of Hawai'i. They believed the patients would live together in true Hawaiian fashion, working the land and adopting one another as family.

There were unexpected complications, however. The settlement got off to a late start, and the first patients didn't have the opportunity to harvest the gardens planted by the people who lived there before them. Bad weather often hampered delivery of government rations. Since medical people, law enforcement officers, and ministers were afraid of leprosy, the patients had very few healthy people to care for them. Some patients brought family members along as helpers, but the government didn't provide rations for these people. So patients ended up sharing their limited supplies.

With so few people to tend to them, Hawaiians with leprosy were disheartened. They felt scared, lonely, and rejected. Instead of living as a community, some thought only of themselves and their own survival. They became lawless and promiscuous, making life even more miserable for the others. This is the story that is most often told about the leprosy settlement.

Even in the midst of the struggles, however, there were faithful people like Keona and her friends who showed kindness and cooperation. Within the first year at the settlement, thirty-five people formed a congregation. They wrote to their friends back on other islands to ask for help in building a church. In the letter they said, "You must not think that all of us are living in sin and degradation. That is not so. Our greatest longing is to make a memorial to God here." A plaque in their church says:

> *Thrust out by mankind*
> *These 12 women and 23 men*
> *Crying aloud to their God*
> *Formed a church*
> *The first in the desolation that was Kalawao.*

This church was the Church of the Healing Spring.

TRUTH OR FICTION?
Healing Water is a fictional account of a real chapter in Hawai'i's history. Pia and Kamaka are fictional, as are most of the characters. However, there are several historical people included in the story.

Mr. Meyer, the administrator of the settlement, lived at the top of the high cliffs that separated the peninsula from the rest of Moloka'i island. He occasionally checked in on Father

Damien, on the *luna*, and on other people in the settlement. The role of *luna* was held by several different people during the years that Pia would have been in the settlement. Hoping to avoid confusing my readers, I chose simply to say *luna*, or boss.

The Reverend Forbes was the American preacher who helped Keona and her Protestant friends form a congregation and bring a church building to Kalawao. He offered moral support and served as a link to the church association in Honolulu. However, it was the faithful Hawaiian believers living in the settlement who made up the Church of the Healing Spring and kept it active in the community.

Pita Kaeo, cousin to Queen Emma, was one of the most prominent Hawaiians sent to Moloka'i with leprosy. The book *News from Molokai,* by Alfons L. Korn, contains the letters Pita and Queen Emma exchanged. Pita arrived about six weeks after Father Damien did, and his letters gave vivid descriptions of life in the leprosy settlement. I included one of his eyewitness accounts in this book—the one about Father Damien weeping because he'd lost the patients' government checks.

There really was a young man named Upa who came to the settlement about the same time as Father Damien. The man who died on the plain was not this Upa, however. As Pia concluded, that man simply represented all the patients who were cast off by the government but cared for by Father Damien.

Bishop Maigret was the Catholic superior who was responsible for the mission in Hawai'i. He was concerned for the residents of Kalawao and visited them occasionally, as he did briefly on the day Father Damien arrived.

FATHER DAMIEN
Father Damien was a Belgian missionary with the Congregation of the Sacred Hearts of Jesus and Mary. He arrived in Hawai'i in 1864, serving first on Hawai'i's largest island. In 1873, when Bishop Maigret asked for a volunteer to go to the Kalawao settlement, the impulsive Damien was quick to accept. Within a short time he decided that the leprosy settlement was his life's work and asked if he could stay there.

Long before this, during the ceremony when Damien became a priest, he had prostrated himself on the chapel floor while other priests lowered a funeral shroud over him. In doing this, he expressed his willingness to die to his own will. In choosing the priesthood, he chose to live and die serving God.

When Father Damien came to Kalawao he brought hope to the people with leprosy. He petitioned the government for money to improve their living conditions. He encouraged recreational activities as well as faith in God. He built coffins and provided burial with dignity. Perhaps the most important thing he did was to touch the people without fear of their disease.

The conversations that Father Damien has with Pia and other invented characters are made up, of course. However, some are based on actual statements he made in letters home. I tried to write all of Damien's dialogue in accordance with his attitudes and personality.

In 1884, Father Damien discovered that he too had leprosy. Even in sickness he continued to work to meet the needs of people like Pia. Stories about him were printed in newspapers around the world. People from many countries heard about his work and sent money and supplies to help out.

On April 15, 1889, at age forty-nine, Father Damien died of complications related to leprosy. His devoted friends buried him beside the small Catholic chapel in Kalawao, under the *hala* tree that had sheltered him on those first nights in the settlement.

He rested peacefully under his tree until 1936, when President Franklin D. Roosevelt granted Belgium's request to have his body returned to his homeland. There he was buried in the town of Leuven at the seminary where he studied to become a priest. Sometime later, when the casket was opened, his remains collapsed from being touched and from the contact with air. They were put into a number of zinc boxes.

The Hawaiian people were heartbroken when the remains of their beloved Father Damien were moved to Belgium; they always felt that at least some part of him should be in Kalawao. So in 1995 the box that contained the remains of his right hand—the hand that had extended so much kindness to the Hawaiian people—was brought back to Hawai'i and buried in his original grave.

In 1969, Hawaiians chose Father Damien as one of two figures to represent their state at the U.S. Capitol building in Washington, DC. The statue erected there shows Father Damien with an advanced case of leprosy.

DAMIEN'S EXAMPLE LIVES ON

Fortunately, Damien's death did not mean the end of kindness in Kalawao. Because of his fearless example, treatment of leprosy patients changed in the settlement. Even before he died, others came to help. The Board of Health sent a resident doctor. A former Civil War soldier, Joseph Dutton, who wanted to make up for some wrongdoings, came and willingly did whatever work Damien gave him. He, too, devoted the rest of his life to the patients there. Catholic nuns came to help care for the girls in the settlement, and more priests came as well. The settlement eventually became known as one of the best leprosy treatment facilities in the whole world. Compassion began to replace isolation and fear.

Much of the fear was unnecessary. We now know that leprosy, which is probably spread when untreated patients cough or sneeze, is not as contagious as we once believed.

THE HAWAIIAN LEPROSY SETTLEMENT TODAY

For over one hundred years, Hawaiians with leprosy were sent to live on Moloka'i. Although the original settlement was in the village of Kalawao, many of the patients lived in caves or built shelters on other parts of the peninsula. As the population on the peninsula increased, the homes moved closer and closer to the non-leprosy village of Kalaupapa on the warmer side. Eventually Kalawao was abandoned, and Kalaupapa, which was more pleasant and comfortable, became the official leprosy village.

Since the 1940s leprosy has been curable with antibiotics. As a result, in 1969 Kalaupapa's residents were finally given the freedom to live wherever they chose. Some left. However, many patients chose to stay because it had become what the Board of Health originally planned—a village of friends looking out for one another.

Many people, especially in the United States, now refer to leprosy as Hansen's Disease. The name comes from Gerhard Hansen, the Norwegian scientist who identified the leprosy germ in 1873.

LEPROSY TODAY

For centuries, people with Hansen's Disease have been referred to as "lepers." This word has many negative ideas and painful feelings attached to it. Although it was used regularly during the time in which this story was set, I chose not to use it. Today it is considered hurtful to call anyone a leper.

The Kalaupapa peninsula is now a National Historical Park. Former patients still live on the sunny western side. From there they travel to other islands or around the world if they want to. They actively speak up for their own rights and for the rights of others affected by Hansen's Disease.

On the cooler eastern side, the old village of Kalawao is little more than lichen-covered rock walls and two small buildings—the Church of the Healing Spring, which was built there first, and Saint Philomena, the Catholic church that Father Damien served.

Father Damien's gravestone is there, as are the graves of countless others—people who were thrust onto the peninsula and who lived out their lives there as best they could.

The Kalaupapa National Historical Park is open for visits because the residents want to share this part of Hawai'i's history. Only people who are at least sixteen years old are allowed to enter. Getting there is not easy. A person can fly in on a small plane, ride down the steep *pali* trail on a mule, or hike down and then up again, as I did. But any of those methods is a small price to pay to visit a spot made sacred by the lives and deaths of so many Hawaiian people.

TIMELINE

1835   The first documented case of leprosy in the Hawaiian islands

1840   Father Damien is born in Belgium as Joseph deVeuster

1864   Father Damien arrives in Hawai'i as a missionary

1866   The first leprosy patients are sent to the Kalaupapa peninsula

1873   Dr. Gerhard Hansen of Norway identifies the leprosy bacillus

Father Damien arrives in the leprosy settlement

1885   A doctor diagnoses Father Damien with leprosy

1889   Father Damien dies of complications caused by leprosy

1936   Father Damien's body is taken from Kalawao to Belgium

1941   First successful drug treatment for leprosy is introduced

1969   Last patient is admitted to Kalaupapa

Patients at Kalaupapa are given freedom to live wherever they choose

1981   United States chooses to use the term *Hansen's Disease* instead of *leprosy*

1995   The remains of Father Damien's right hand are returned to his grave in Kalawao

ABOUT HAWAIIAN

Pia's story is set at a time when many changes were coming to Hawai'i. As the influence of Western ways and the English language grew, the Hawaiian language and culture were overwhelmed and suppressed.

Fortunately, Hawaiian people decided to reclaim their heritage, a process highlighted by a "Hawaiian Renaissance," a return to cultural practices, in the early 1970s. In 1978 a law was passed that made Hawaiian an official state language along with English. Today, there are many programs and resources for learning this beautiful language and ensuring its perpetuation.

A FEW FACTS ABOUT HAWAIIAN

Hawaiian contains five vowels: *a* (pronounced *ah*, as in "father"), *e* (*eh*, as in "red"), *i* (*ee*, as in "pita"), *o* (*oh*, as in "home"), and *u* (*oo*, as in "tuna"). Every syllable must end in a vowel.

A Hawaiian word does not have to have a consonant. There are eight consonants: *h* (*heh*), *k* (*keh*), *l* (*lah*), *m* (*moo*), *n* (*noo*), *p* (*peh*), *w* (*veh*), and the 'okina (*oh-kee-nah*), which is written with a backward apostrophe: '.

The 'okina is what linguists call a glottal stop. When you see the ' in a Hawaiian word, you cut off the sound before voicing the next vowel. O'o would be pronounced *oh-oh*.

Many Hawaiian words that once used the 'okina are commonly expressed without it now. The words Hawaii (Hawai'i), Molokai (Moloka'i), and Oahu (O'ahu) are examples. In some words, however, the 'okina cannot be left out without changing the meaning. For example, *pau* means "end" or "finish"; *pa'u* means "soot." That one mark makes a big difference! All Hawaiian words, including place names, have been spelled the authentic way in this book.

Words do not have silent letters—all letters are pronounced.

A *kahakō* (or macron) is a line over a vowel—as there is over the *o* in *kahakō*—to show that it should be elongated.

GLOSSARY

aloha   love, hello, greetings, goodbye

auē   (often spelled *auwē*) an exclamation of grief or surprise, "Alas!"

hala   a common tree (also called pandanus) that sends roots down from its branches; its leaves are used for weaving mats and other household items

haole   a foreigner, particularly an American or a European

hapa haole   a person who is part Hawaiian and part foreigner

Hawai'i   the name of a group of islands and also the name of the largest island in the group

kalo   taro, Hawai'i's most important plant, used for food, medicine, and much more

kī   (sometimes called *tī*) a plant used for medicinal and household purposes, believed to bring good luck and ward off spirits; food was often wrapped or served in *kī* leaves

Kīlauea   the name of the active volcano on the "Big Island" of Hawai'i

koa   a large, strong tree valued for its lumber

kōkua   helper, attendant

Kona   an overwhelming leeward wind

kukui   a tree that produces nuts with an oily substance inside that was used for lamps

lānai   porch

lau hala   leaf of the *hala* tree

lei   garland

lūʻau a Hawaiian feast

luna overseer, boss

Pele the goddess of fire who lives in the volcanoes

maile a vine with sweet-smelling leaves used for making flower garlands

makai toward the sea

māmaki a plant used to make herbal tea

Māui one of Hawaiʻi's ancient gods, known for superhuman strength and mischief; Maui (without a macron) is the name of one of the Hawaiian islands

mauka inland, toward the mountain

Menehune legendary little people who came out at night and accomplished difficult tasks for the people of Hawaiʻi

Molokaʻi the name of a Hawaiian island

noni a shrub or small tree; the bitter fruit was often used medicinally, and the roots were used for dyes

Oʻahu the name of the most populous of the Hawaiian islands; Pia's home was there

ʻohana extended family

pali a cliff or precipice

poi a thick paste made by cooking and mashing the taro root, traditionally eaten at every meal

pōpoki cat

pōpolo an important medicinal plant used for cuts, wounds, and respiratory ailments

tūtū grandparent, or a relative or close friend from the grandparents' generation

RESOURCES

I first learned about Father Damien in 1996. His story touched me, and I quickly realized I wanted to write about it. In the years since, at times when some daily task has seemed too difficult, Damien's example has often inspired me to accept the challenge.

Much has been written about Father Damien. Some of it is certainly exaggerated, but one cannot overstate how much his compassion touched the people of Hawai'i and how widely his influence spread throughout the world.

The resources I learned from include:

BOOKS

Father Damien: A Journey from Cashmere to His Home in Hawaii, by Edward Clifford (Macmillan, 1890)

The Gift of Pain, by Paul Brand and Philip Yancey (Zondervan, 1997)

Gifts from the Shore: A Kalaupapa Diary, by Roberta M. Jarrett (Pacific Editions, 1993)

Hawaii and Its People, by A. Grove Day (Meredith Press, 1955)

The Hawaiians, by Robert B. Goodman, Gavan Daws, and Ed Sheehan (Island Heritage Limited, 1970)

The Heart of Father Damien, by Vital Jourdain, SS.CC. (Bruce Publishing, 1955)

History of the Catholic Mission in the Hawaiian Islands, by Father Reginald Yzendoorn, SS.CC. (Honolulu Star-Bulletin, 1927)

Holy Man: Father Damien of Molokai, by Gavan Daws (University of Hawaii Press, 1973)

Honolulu: Sketches of Life in the Hawaiian Islands from 1828–1861, by Laura Fish Judd (Lakeside Press, R. R. Donnelley and Sons, 1966)

Kalaupapa and the Legacy of Father Damien, by Anwei V. Skinsnes Law and Richard A. Wisniewski (Pacific Basin Enterprises, 1988)

Lā'au Hawai'i: Traditional Hawaiian Uses of Plants, by Isabella Aiona Abbott (Bishop Museum Press, 1992)

The Lepers of Molokai, by Charles Warren Stoddard (Ave Maria Press, 1885)

Life and Letters of Father Damien, the Apostle of the Lepers, by Father Pamphile (Catholic Truth Society, 1889)

The Lymans of Hilo: A Fascinating Account of Life in 19ᵗʰ Century Hawaii, by Margaret Greer Martin (Lyman House Memorial Museum, 1979)

Molokai, by O. A. Bushnell (historical fiction) (World Publishing Company, 1963; University of Hawaii Press, 1975)

News from Molokai: Letters Between Peter Kaeo and Queen Emma, 1873–1876, Edited by Alfons L. Korn (University of Hawaii Press, 1976)

Olivia: My Life of Exile in Kalaupapa, by Olivia Robello Breitha (Arizona Memorial Museum Association, 1988)

The Path of the Destroyer: A History of Leprosy in the Hawaiian Islands and Thirty Years' Research into the Means By Which It Has Been Spread, by Arthur A. Mouritz (Honolulu Star-Bulletin, 1916)

Pilgrimage and Exile: Mother Marianne of Molokai, by Sister Mary Laurence Hanley, O.S.F. and O. A. Bushnell (University of Hawaii Press, 1991)

A Portrait of Molokai, by James H. Brocker (Molokai Fish and Dive Corporation, 1994)

Shoal of Time: A History of the Hawaiian Islands, by Gavan Daws (Macmillan, 1968)

Siloama: The Church of the Healing Spring, by Ethel M. Damon (Hawaiian Board of Missions, 1948)

Six Months in the Sandwich Islands, by Isabella L. Bird (G. P. Putnam's Sons, 1881; Mutual Publishing, 1998)

BOOKS OF INTEREST TO YOUNG PEOPLE

Ancient Hawai'i, by Herb Kawainui Kāne (Kawainui Press, 1997)

Father Damien and the Bells, by A. T. Sheehan and Elizabeth Odell Sheehan (Ignatius Press, 2004)

Hawaiian Journey, by Joseph G. Mullins (Mutual Publishing, 1978)

In the Shadow of the Pali, by Lisa Cindrich (historical fiction) (Putnam Juvenile Books, 2002)

Kalaupapa: A Portrait, by Wayne Levin and Anwei Skinsnes Law (Arizona Memorial Museum Association and Bishop Museum Press, 1989)

The Lands of Father Damien: Kalaupapa, Molokai, Hawaii, by James H. Brocker (Kaunakakai, Molokai: James H. Brocker, 1997)

Learn Hawaiian at Home, by Kahikāhealani Wight (CDs and book) (Bess Press, 2005)

Tales of the Menehune, by Mary Kawena Pūku'i and Caroline Curtis (Kamehameha Schools Press, 1960)

Yesterday at Kalaupapa, by Emmett Cahill (Editions Limited, 1990)

DVDs AND AUDIO

Molokai: The Story of Father Damien (DVD), directed by Paul Cox (ERA Films, 2003)

Tales of a Hawaiian Boyhood: The Kalaupapa Years (audio), by Makia Malo (Makia and Ann Malo, 1993)

An Uncommon Kindness: The Father Damien Story (DVD), narrated by Robin Williams (Blue Rider Production, 2003)

WEB SITES*

www.leprosy.org — site of American Leprosy Missions

www.idealeprosydignity.org — Web site of IDEA, International Organization for Integration, Dignity and Economic Advancement

*Active at the time of publication.

www.aoc.gov/cc/art/nsh/damien.cfm — Web site of National Statuary Hall collection, with information about Father Damien statue

www.damien-duttonleprosysociety.org — a nonprofit organization that seeks to conquer leprosy

www.visitmolokai.com/kala — Hawaiian site with information about the Kalaupapa peninsula

bphc.hrsa.gov/NHDP/NHD_MUSEUM_HISTORY — site of the National Hansen's Disease Museum (in Carville, LA, where the United States sent its leprosy patients for over one hundred years)

PLACES TO VISIT

Damien Museum, Honolulu, Oʻahu, Hawaiʻi (130 Ohua Avenue, Honolulu, HI 96815)

Kalaupapa National Historical Park, Kalaupapa, Molokaʻi, Hawaiʻi (visitors must be at least 16 years old) (*www.nps.gov/kala*)

Statues of Father Damien: Honolulu, Oʻahu, Hawaiʻi, and in the Statuary Hall of the U.S. Capitol Building, Washington, DC

Damien Birthplace Museum, Pater Damiaanstraat 37, Tremeloo, Belgium (e-mail: *damiaanmuseum@gmail.com*)

The National Hansen's Disease Museum, 5445 Point Clair Road, Carville, LA 70721

Mahalo Nui
[A BIG THANK YOU]

To my editor, Carolyn Yoder, for waiting patiently while I struggled to find Pia's voice. Because of you he speaks more eloquently and I write more clearly.

To Katya Rice, copyeditor extraordinaire, for bringing precision to the details and clarity to the big picture.

To Helen Robinson, for another amazing book design!

To the entire staff of Calkins Creek Books and Boyds Mills Press, for the work you do that I will never know about.

To the librarians who accessed out-of-print titles for me, especially those at the Quarryville/Lancaster County (PA) Library.

To Dr. Harold and Miriam Housman, Dr. Richard F. Keeler, and Dr. Chris Leuz, for reviewing the manuscript and sharing your expertise regarding leprosy.

To Anwei Skinsnes Law, for urging me to look beyond the traditional telling of Hawai'i's leprosy history. Your candor and compassion pushed me to discover the spirit of *aloha* that helped so many to survive in Kalaupapa.

To Rick Caceres and Michelle Wee, for reading the manuscript with Hawaiian eyes and letting me know how it worked.

To Keoni Kelekolio, for your help with the Hawaiian language and for answering questions related to Hawaiian culture.

To Roberta M. Jarrett, for your tender reflections and vivid descriptions of Kalawao and Kalaupapa.

To David W. Hains, for feedback regarding the Catholic components of the story.

To Father Paul Macken, SS.CC., for the wonderful tour you gave us of Father Damien's birthplace and his crypt, and for answering many questions regarding his life and religious practice.

To Rick, Ruth, Marilyn, and Kelby, for reading the story long before it was truly readable.

To Elma and Wendy, for hiking the Kalaupapa trail with me— and for spending so much of the Hawai'i trip in museums and so little of it on the beach. Isn't research fun?

To my husband, Chuck, for sending me on research trips to faraway places. And especially for sharing the journey!

To each of you, *aloha nui loa*—much love and goodwill!